P9-CJJ-195

JOURNEY UNDER THE ARCTIC

Also in the
Fabien Cousteau Expeditions

GREAT WHITE SHARK ADVENTURE

JOURNEY UNDER THE ARCTIC

WRITTEN BY
JAMES O. FRAIOLI

ILLUSTRATED BY
JOE ST.PIERRE

MARGARET K. McELDERRY BOOKS
NEW YORK LONDON TORONTO SYDNEY NEW DELHI

AUTHORS' NOTE

Journey under the Arctic is a work of fiction based on actual expeditions and accepted ideas about the Arctic and its inhabitants.

MARGARET K. McELDERRY BOOKS
An imprint of Simon & Schuster Children's Publishing Division
1230 Avenue of the Americas, New York, New York 10020

For information about special discounts for bulk purchases, please contact Simon & Schuster Special Sales at 1-866-506-1949 or business@simonandschuster.com.
The Simon & Schuster Speakers Bureau can bring authors to your live event. For more information or to book an event, contact the Simon & Schuster Speakers Bureau at 1-866-248-3049 or visit our website at www.simonspeakers.com.
Also available in a Margaret K. McElderry Books paper-over-board edition
Book design by Sonia Chaghatzbanian
The text for this book was set in Wild and Crazy.
The illustrations for this book were rendered digitally.
Manufactured in China
1219 SCP
First Margaret K. McElderry Books hardcover edition March 2020
10 9 8 7 6 5 4 3 2 1
Library of Congress Cataloging-in-Publication Data
Names: Fraioli, James O., 1968– author. | St. Pierre, Joe, illustrator. | Cousteau, Fabien.
Title: Journey under the Arctic / written by James O. Fraioli ; illustrated by Joe St. Pierre.
Description: First edition. | New York, New York : Margaret K. McElderry Books, [2020] | Series: [Fabien Cousteau expeditions ; 2] | Audience: Ages 8–12. | Audience: Grades 4–6. | Summary: Junior explorers Rocco and Olivia join Fabien Cousteau and his research team on an icebreaker in the Arctic Circle, seeking the rare dumbo octopus. Inserts include facts about the effects of climate change, people and animals of the Arctic, and ships that have explored the area.
Identifiers: LCCN 2019041176 (print) | ISBN 9781534420908 (paper-over-board) | ISBN 9781534420915 (hardcover) | ISBN 9781534420922 (eBook)
Subjects: LCSH: Graphic novels. | CYAC: Graphic novels. | Octopuses—Fiction. | Rare animals—Fiction. | Cousteau, Fabien, Fiction. | Scientists—Fiction. | Arctic regions—Fiction.
Classification: LCC PZ7.7.F72 Jou 2020 (print) | DDC [Fic]—dc23
LC record available at https://lccn.loc.gov/2019041176

JOURNEY UNDER THE ARCTIC

SOMEWHERE IN THE ARCTIC OCEAN, *1775*
ON DECK! SHIP AHEAD!
SHE LOOKS BADLY BEATEN.
OCTAVIUS
HER FROSTED SAILS ARE TATTERED AND TORN... BARELY HANGING ON THE MASTS. MIGHT SHE BE DESERTED?
PREPARE A BOARDING PARTY.
AYE, CAPTAIN.

OH MY GOD
IN HEAVEN...

CAPTAIN,
IN HERE!

DEATH AS WELL.
COLLECT THE SHIP'S LOG.
"WE TRIED TO NAVIGATE THE NORTHWEST PASSAGE, BUT OUR SHIP HAS BECOME IMPRISONED..."

We tried to navigate the Northwest Passage, but our ship has become imprisoned in the ice-choked sea of the Arctic... Our fire has gone out and our master has tried to light it, but has failed. It doesn't matter... We no longer feel cold

WHAT SHOULD WE DO WITH THE SHIP AND HER CREW?

NOTHING. I FEAR THE *OCTAVIUS* IS CURSED.

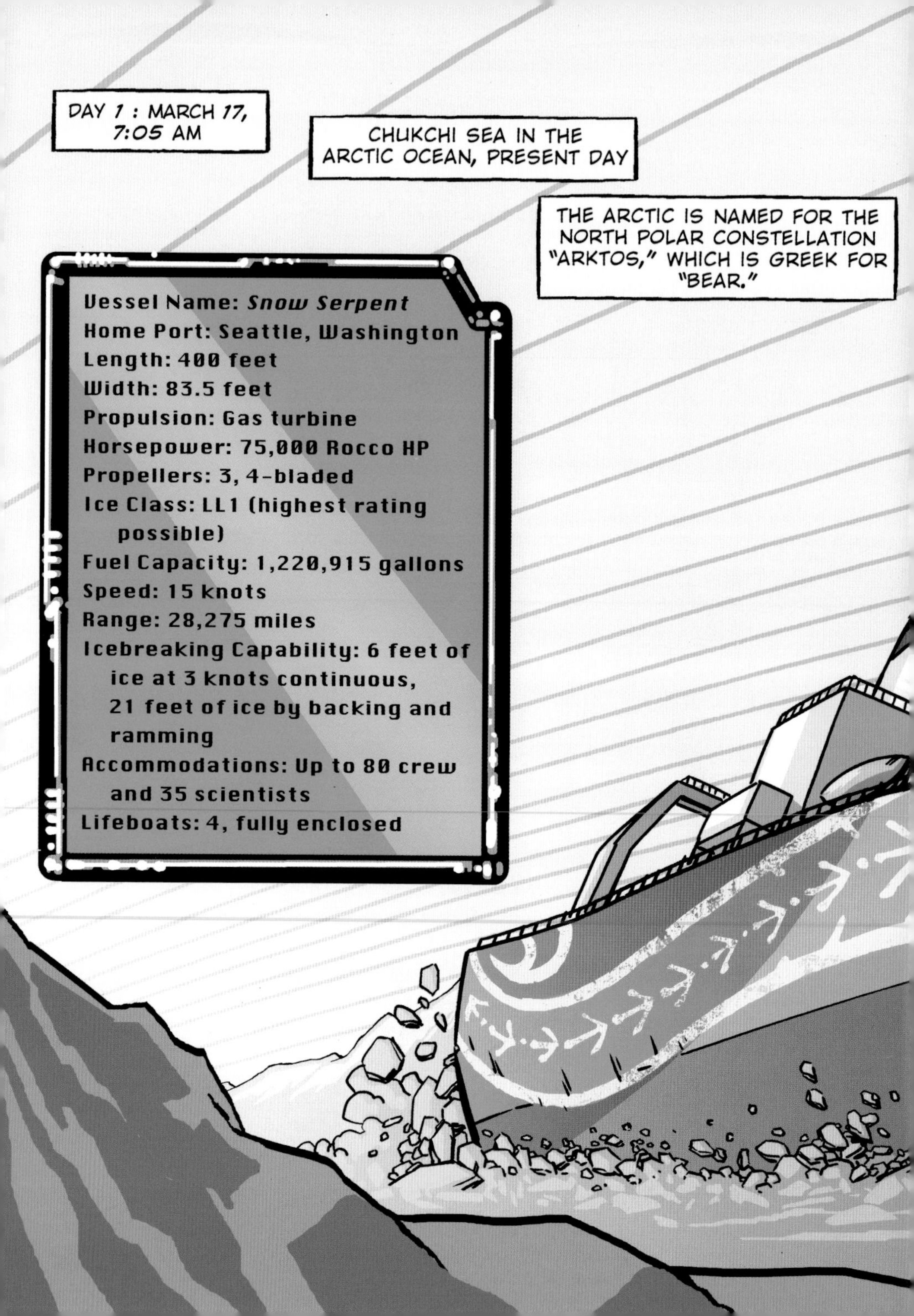

DAY 1 : MARCH 17, 7:05 AM

CHUKCHI SEA IN THE ARCTIC OCEAN, PRESENT DAY

THE ARCTIC IS NAMED FOR THE NORTH POLAR CONSTELLATION "ARKTOS," WHICH IS GREEK FOR "BEAR."

Vessel Name: *Snow Serpent*
Home Port: Seattle, Washington
Length: 400 feet
Width: 83.5 feet
Propulsion: Gas turbine
Horsepower: 75,000 Rocco HP
Propellers: 3, 4-bladed
Ice Class: LL1 (highest rating possible)
Fuel Capacity: 1,220,915 gallons
Speed: 15 knots
Range: 28,275 miles
Icebreaking Capability: 6 feet of ice at 3 knots continuous, 21 feet of ice by backing and ramming
Accommodations: Up to 80 crew and 35 scientists
Lifeboats: 4, fully enclosed

ICEBREAKERS ARE USED TO REACH PLACES WHERE SEVERE ICE CONDITIONS FORBID OTHER VESSELS FROM SAILING. THE FIRST SUCCESSFUL ICEBREAKERS WERE BUILT IN RUSSIA IN THE MID-1800S.

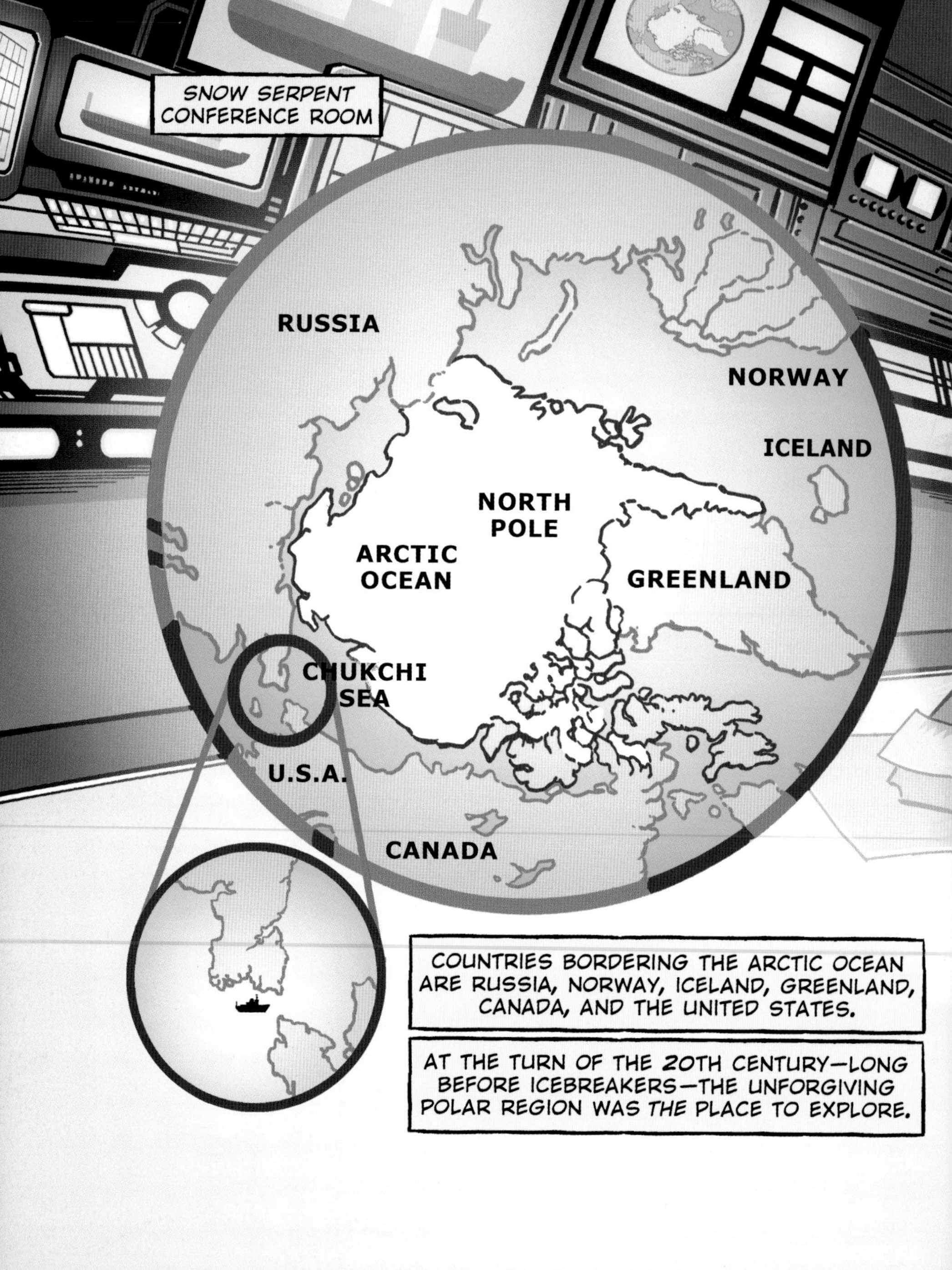

COUNTRIES BORDERING THE ARCTIC OCEAN ARE RUSSIA, NORWAY, ICELAND, GREENLAND, CANADA, AND THE UNITED STATES.

AT THE TURN OF THE 20TH CENTURY—LONG BEFORE ICEBREAKERS—THE UNFORGIVING POLAR REGION WAS *THE* PLACE TO EXPLORE.

WELCOME ABOARD THE SNOW SERPENT!
la: 69.4713 North
lo: 171.6903 West
la: 90.000 North
lo: 135.000 West
FABIEN COUSTEAU
EXPEDITION LEADER
FABIEN COUSTEAU HAS SPENT HIS LIFE TREKKING ACROSS THE GLOBE, INVESTIGATING THE WORLD'S OCEANS AND THEIR UNUSUAL AND BIZARRE INHABITANTS, JUST LIKE HIS GRANDFATHER, THE LEGENDARY JACQUES-YVES COUSTEAU.

THIS SHIP IS ONE OF THE MOST ADVANCED ICEBREAKERS IN THE WORLD. SHE'S PERFECTLY DESIGNED FOR NAVIGATING THROUGH THE ARCTIC, WHICH HAPPENS TO BE ONE OF THE COLDEST OCEANS ON THE PLANET.

ROCCO & OLIVIA
JUNIOR EXPEDITIONERS

La: 90.000 North
Lo: 135.000 West

GLORIA PEREZ
MARINE BIOLOGIST

MATT CHAN
EXPLORATION SUPERVISOR

THE ARCTIC OCEAN IS SO COLD, IT DEVELOPS A THICK LAYER OF SEA ICE ON THE SURFACE DURING MOST OF THE YEAR.

BECAUSE OF THE HIGH SALT CONTENT, OCEAN WATER IN THE ARCTIC FREEZES AT 29°F.

THE *SNOW SERPENT*, UNLIKE *TITANIC*, HAS A REINFORCED HULL AND PROTECTED PROPELLERS AND RUDDER.
SHE HAS ENOUGH MUSCLE TO RAM HER WAY THROUGH ICE MORE THAN 20 FEET THICK.

THE FAMOUS PASSENGER SHIP *TITANIC* STRUCK A LARGE ICEBERG THAT DRIFTED FROM THE ARCTIC AND SANK THE VESSEL IN THE EARLY MORNING HOURS ON APRIL 15, 1912.

HI, TEAM, IT'S THE CAPTAIN. PLEASE SWITCH ON THE VIDEO CONFERENCE SCREEN.
THERE'S A MESSAGE COMING IN FOR YOU.
COPY THAT, CAP.

HI, FABIEN! HI, GUYS!
HELLO, KIDS!
WE WOULD JUST LIKE TO WISH EVERYONE A SUCCESSFUL EXPEDITION UP IN THE ARCTIC!
THANK YOU!

WE WOULD ALSO LIKE TO LET YOU KNOW THAT BELLA, THE MONSTER SHARK WE TAGGED IN SOUTH AFRICA, IS DOING GREAT AND MIGRATING A LONG DISTANCE. SHE WAS LAST SPOTTED OFF THE NEPTUNE ISLANDS IN SOUTH AUSTRALIA.

THAT'S WONDERFUL NEWS! THANK YOU!

THE LARGEST KNOWN ICEBERG, REPORTED BY A UNITED STATES COAST GUARD ICEBREAKER IN *1957*, MEASURED MORE THAN *550* FEET TALL, ABOUT THE SAME HEIGHT AS A *55*-STORY BUILDING.

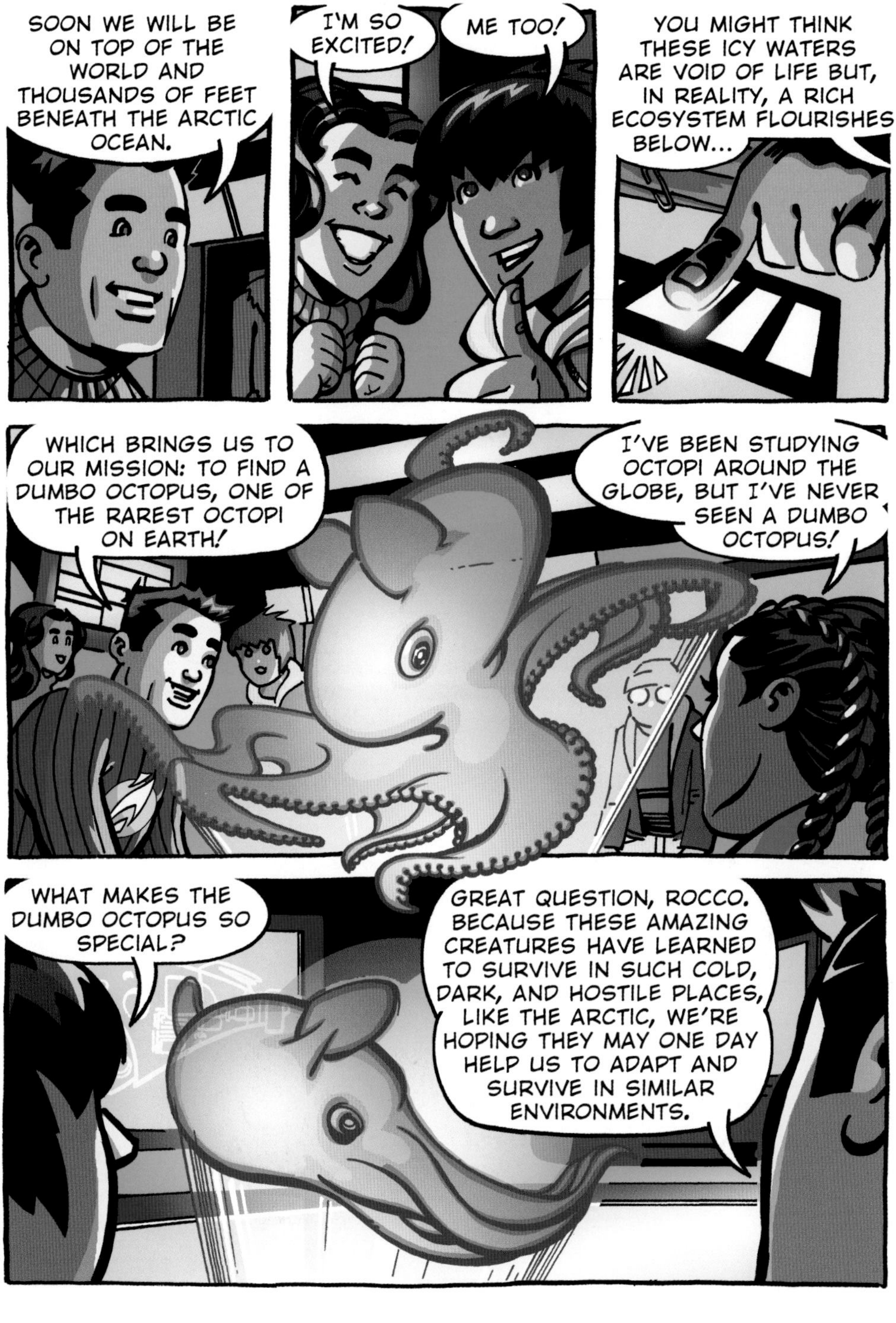

SOON WE WILL BE ON TOP OF THE WORLD AND THOUSANDS OF FEET BENEATH THE ARCTIC OCEAN.

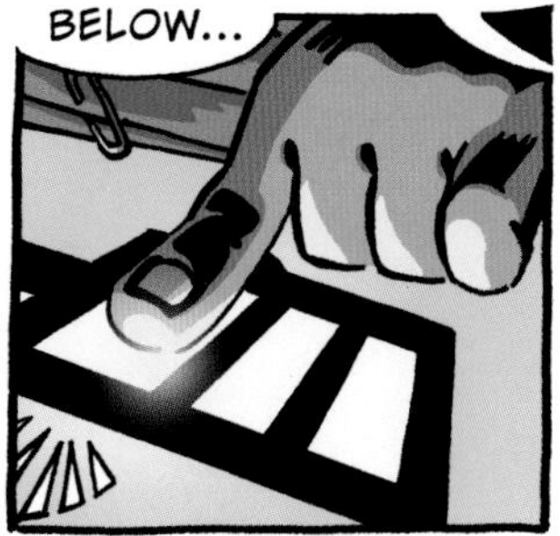

WHICH BRINGS US TO OUR MISSION: TO FIND A DUMBO OCTOPUS, ONE OF THE RAREST OCTOPI ON EARTH!

I'VE BEEN STUDYING OCTOPI AROUND THE GLOBE, BUT I'VE NEVER SEEN A DUMBO OCTOPUS!

WHAT MAKES THE DUMBO OCTOPUS SO SPECIAL?

GREAT QUESTION, ROCCO. BECAUSE THESE AMAZING CREATURES HAVE LEARNED TO SURVIVE IN SUCH COLD, DARK, AND HOSTILE PLACES, LIKE THE ARCTIC, WE'RE HOPING THEY MAY ONE DAY HELP US TO ADAPT AND SURVIVE IN SIMILAR ENVIRONMENTS.

FROM WHAT I HEAR, THESE OCTOPI ARE EXTREMELY INTELLIGENT AND VERY DIFFICULT TO FIND.
THEY ARE, INDEED. UNLIKE THE OCTOPI WE COMMONLY SEE IN AQUARIUMS, THIS PARTICULAR ANIMAL IS SELDOM ENCOUNTERED AND OFTEN FOUND IN THE DEEPEST REACHES OF THE SEA.
AS YOU CAN SEE FROM THESE IMAGES, THE DUMBO OCTOPUS LOOKS MORE LIKE A CHILD'S TOY.
THE DUMBO OCTOPUS, LIKE OTHER OCTOPI, HAS EIGHT ARMS AND LARGE EYES.
WHAT SEPARATES IT FROM OTHER SPECIES IS THE UNUSUAL FINS ON THE SIDE OF ITS HEAD, WHICH IT FLAPS LIKE THE CARTOON CHARACTER DUMBO, THE FLYING ELEPHANT.
THAT'S HOW IT GOT ITS NAME.
VERY COOL!

THE LARGEST DUMBO OCTOPUS EVER RECORDED MEASURED ALMOST 6 FEET IN LENGTH AND WEIGHED 13 POUNDS.

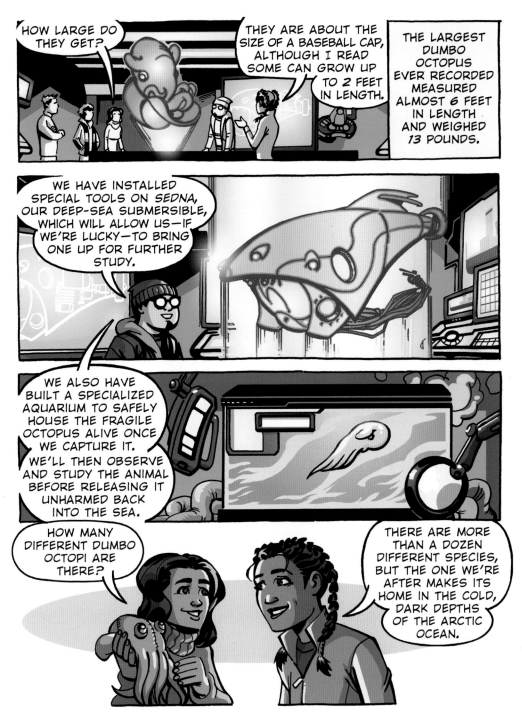

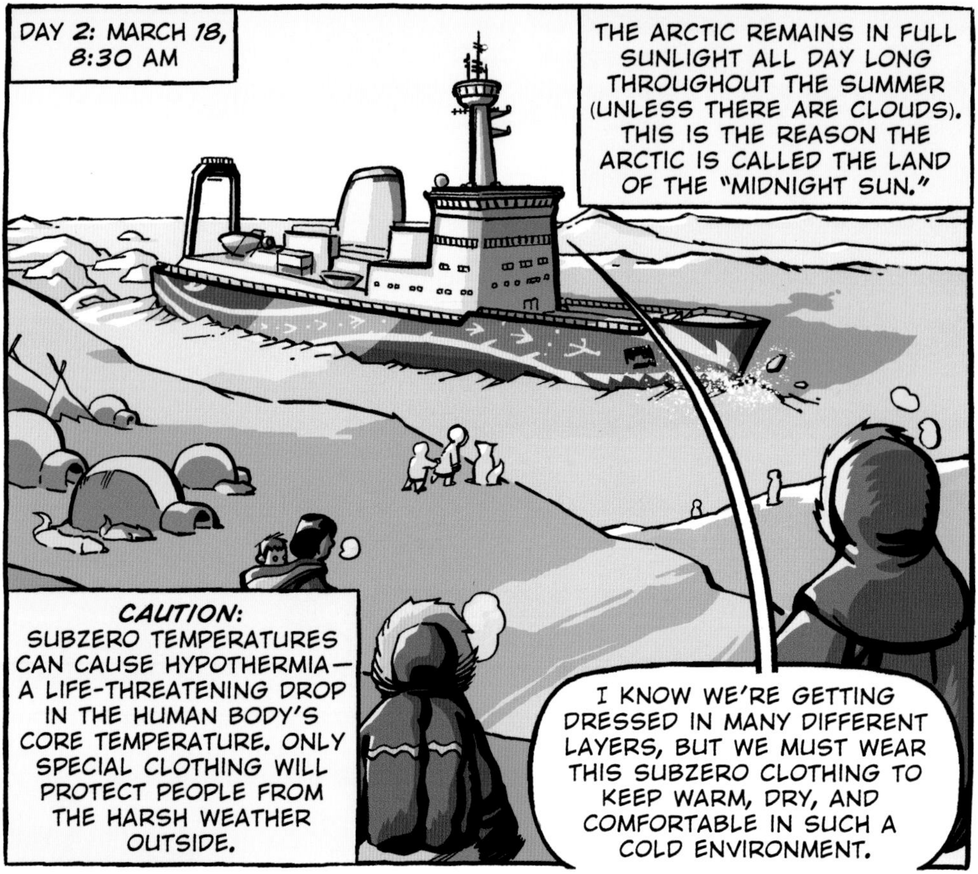

DAY 2: MARCH 18, 8:30 AM

THE ARCTIC REMAINS IN FULL SUNLIGHT ALL DAY LONG THROUGHOUT THE SUMMER (UNLESS THERE ARE CLOUDS). THIS IS THE REASON THE ARCTIC IS CALLED THE LAND OF THE "MIDNIGHT SUN."

CAUTION: SUBZERO TEMPERATURES CAN CAUSE HYPOTHERMIA—A LIFE-THREATENING DROP IN THE HUMAN BODY'S CORE TEMPERATURE. ONLY SPECIAL CLOTHING WILL PROTECT PEOPLE FROM THE HARSH WEATHER OUTSIDE.

I KNOW WE'RE GETTING DRESSED IN MANY DIFFERENT LAYERS, BUT WE MUST WEAR THIS SUBZERO CLOTHING TO KEEP WARM, DRY, AND COMFORTABLE IN SUCH A COLD ENVIRONMENT.

THESE SUITS INCLUDE A HEATING SYSTEM THAT'S MADE OUT OF THE CARBON AND SILVER INK PRINTED ON THEM.
THE FLEXIBLE INK CONDUCTS HEAT AND IS BONDED TO THE INSIDE.
THE HEAT IS CONTROLLED BY A SLIM BATTERY PACK AND CAN BE ADJUSTED TO A HIGH OR LOW SETTING.
IT LASTS UP TO 5 HOURS AT THE HIGHEST SETTING AND 11 HOURS AT THE LOWEST.
THE BUTTONS ON THE BATTERY PACK ARE EXTRA LARGE SO WE CAN PUSH THEM WITH OUR GLOVES ON.
Arctic Hat
Sunglasses
Thermal Base Layer
Thermal Mid/ Outer Layer
HOW COOL IS THAT?
Down Gloves
Deluxe Anti-Exposure Work Suit (with heating system)
THIS UNIQUE HEATING SYSTEM WAS FIRST INTRODUCED DURING THE WINTER OLYMPICS IN SOUTH KOREA TO COMBAT THE BITTER COLD.
Snowshoe Boots
Snowshoes

THAT'S RIGHT! AND REMEMBER, THE ARCTIC OCEAN MAY BE THE SMALLEST AND SHALLOWEST OF THE WORLD'S FIVE MAJOR OCEANS, BUT DON'T LET ITS SIZE FOOL YOU.

THIS OCEAN IS ALMOST THE SIZE OF NORTH AMERICA.

THE ARCTIC OCEAN COVERS 5.4 MILLION SQUARE MILES AND IS LARGER THAN EUROPE. IT'S ALSO CONNECTED TO THE PACIFIC OCEAN BY THE BERING STRAIT AND TO THE ATLANTIC OCEAN BY THE GREENLAND SEA.

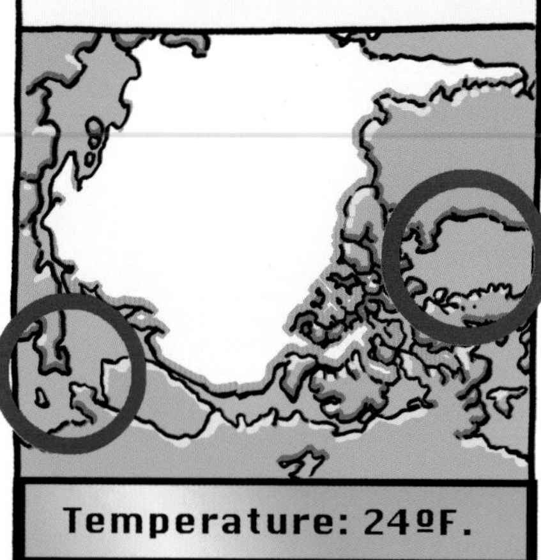

Temperature: 24ºF.

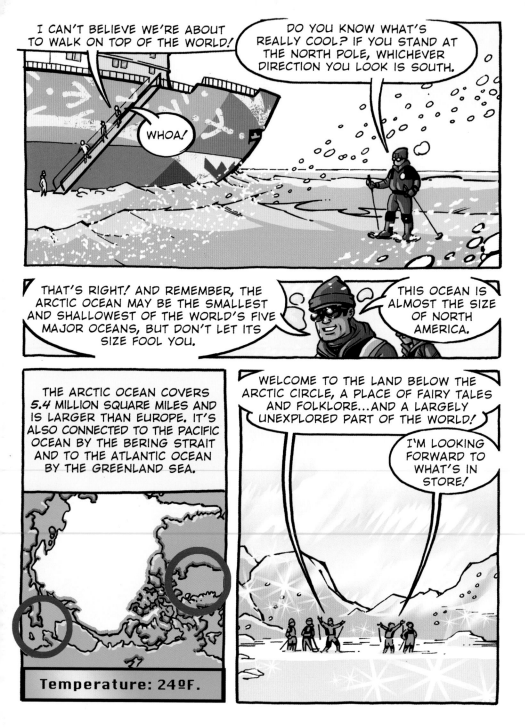

WHY IS THAT LITTLE TUGBOAT TOWING THAT GINORMOUS ICEBERG?
IT'S TO MELT INTO DRINKING WATER.
ARE YOU SERIOUS?
ABSOLUTELY. DO YOU KNOW THERE ARE MORE THAN 1 BILLION PEOPLE IN THE WORLD WITHOUT CLEAN DRINKING WATER?
NO, I DIDN'T KNOW THAT. I JUST THOUGHT WE ALL HAD CLEAN DRINKING WATER.
IF ONLY THAT WERE TRUE.
FABIEN'S RIGHT. WITH MANY PEOPLE IN THE WORLD WITHOUT FRESH, CLEAN WATER, AND WITH BILLIONS OF GALLONS OF FRESHWATER DISAPPEARING USELESSLY INTO THE OCEAN FROM MELTING ICEBERGS, IT SEEMS THESE FLOATING BERGS COULD SERVE A GREATER PURPOSE.
ABSOLUTELY. AND BECAUSE ICEBERGS ARE THE RESULT OF PIECES OF GLACIAL ICE BREAKING FREE AND FALLING INTO THE SEA, THEY CONTAIN 12,000-YEAR-OLD FRESHWATER AND LIKELY THE PUREST WATER ON THE PLANET.

POLAR SEA ICE IS FROZEN SEAWATER, WHILE ICEBERGS ARE FROZEN FRESHWATER THAT COME FROM GLACIERS ON THE LANDS SURROUNDING THE ARCTIC OCEAN.
HOW FAR DO THEY HAVE TO TOW THE ICEBERG?
THAT'S THE TRICK—TO TOW IT ACROSS THE OCEAN BEFORE IT MELTS.
THAT'S WHAT THAT TALL FENCE-LIKE BELT IS THAT YOU CAN SEE STRAPPED AROUND THE ICEBERG. IT'S ACTUALLY CALLED A FLOATING GEOTEXTILE BELT.
IT ACTS AS A BARRIER TO KEEP OUT WAVES THAT MIGHT ERODE THE ICEBERG, WHILE BELOW IS A GEOTEXTILE SKIRT THAT WRAPS AROUND THE ICEBERG LIKE A CURTAIN AND PROTECTS IT FROM STRONG OCEAN CURRENTS BELOW THAT MAY DAMAGE THE PRECIOUS CARGO.
AND IF THEY'RE ABLE TO KEEP TOWING THE ICEBERGS SUCCESSFULLY TO THEIR DESTINATION, MAYBE ONE DAY THE ARCTIC WILL SOLVE GLOBAL THIRST BY SUPPLYING ABUNDANT FRESHWATER TO THE ENTIRE WORLD.

HEY, WHAT ARE THOSE BIRDS OVER THERE?
THOSE ARE ARCTIC PUFFINS. THEIR LATIN NAME IS *FRATERCULA ARCTICA,* WHICH MEANS "LITTLE BROTHER OF THE NORTH."
PERHAPS THEIR COMMON NAME, "CLOWNS OF THE AIR," IS MORE APPROPRIATE, AS PUFFINS LIKE TO HAVE FUN, SUCH AS JOY FLYING AND DIVEBOMBING.
UNFORTUNATELY, THEIR FEEDING HABITS AREN'T AS FUN.
WHAT DO YOU MEAN?
INSTEAD OF DINING ON COLD, RICH ARCTIC FISH LIKE POLAR COD, MOST OF THESE PUFFINS, AND MANY OTHER FORAGING ARCTIC SEABIRDS FOR THAT MATTER, ARE NOW FINDING THEMSELVES EATING LESS NUTRITIOUS CREATURES MORE AT HOME IN THE WARMER ATLANTIC.

THAT'S RIGHT. THE SEA IS CHANGING AS WARM ATLANTIC WATERS MUSCLE THEIR WAY INTO THE ARCTIC OCEAN, LEAVING OUR SEABIRDS CRITICALLY SHORT ON FUEL.
WHY IS THAT?
IT'S BECAUSE THE ICE IS MELTING AT AN ALARMING RATE, CAUSING THE ARCTIC OCEAN TO BE DILUTED WITH FRESHWATER. IN TURN, THIS WEAKENS THE SEAWATER, MAKING IT EASIER FOR WARMER OCEANS LIKE THE ATLANTIC TO MOVE IN AND MIX WITH THE ARCTIC WHILE RAISING THE WATER TEMPERATURE.
IF ALL THE ICE IN THE ARCTIC MELTED, THE GLOBAL SEA LEVEL WOULD RISE 24 FEET.
THE MORE THE ICE SHRINKS, THE MORE ATLANTIC WATER CAN MOVE IN.
WHAT'S CAUSING THE ICE TO MELT SO FAST?
CARBON DIOXIDE.
O
C
O
IT'S ENTERING THE EARTH'S ATMOSPHERE IN VERY LARGE AMOUNTS, WHICH IS WHY THE ARCTIC ALSO HAPPENS TO BE ONE OF THE MOST THREATENED PLACES ON EARTH.

AND WHY WE NEED TO FIND WAYS TO REDUCE THE CARBON DIOXIDE THAT'S BEING EMITTED.
FABIEN'S RIGHT. THE MORE WE CAN REDUCE OUR CARBON FOOTPRINT, THE BETTER WE CAN MAKE THE WORLD FOR FUTURE GENERATIONS.
I STILL CAN'T BELIEVE WE'RE SNOWSHOEING OVER AN OCEAN!
DIFFICULT TO IMAGINE, ISN'T IT?
WE'RE PROBABLY OFF THE OCEAN BY NOW, SEEING THAT WE ANCHORED ON THE EDGE AND SHOULD NOW BE OVER THE FROZEN SHORELINE.
IF YOU HAVEN'T NOTICED, THERE AREN'T ANY TREES UP HERE.
HOW COME?
BECAUSE TREES CAN'T SURVIVE IN THE ARCTIC DUE TO THE EXTREME LOW TEMPERATURES HIGH WINDS, AND LACK OF RAIN UP HERE.
THE AREA WHERE THE TREES STOP GROWING IS CALLED THE "TREE LINE."

SOME RESEARCHERS CONSIDER THAT LINE TO BE WHERE THE ARCTIC BEGINS AND ENDS.

WHOA, IS THAT A RABBIT?

A POLAR RABBIT, ALSO KNOWN AS AN ARCTIC HARE. THEY'VE ADAPTED TO THE EXTREME COLD BY HAVING SMALL EARS, LIMBS, AND NOSES, AND VERY THICK FUR.

ARCTIC

TREE LINE

THE ARCTIC HARE CAN RUN UP TO 40 MILES PER HOUR. IT'S GOOD TO HAVE THAT KIND OF SPEED WHEN BEING CHASED BY PREDATORS, WHICH INCLUDE THE ARCTIC FOX, ARCTIC WOLF, AND SNOWY OWL.

HOW ARE YOU KIDS DOING IN THIS COLD?
I'M DOING GREAT! I LIKE ALL OF THIS SNOWSHOEING.
ME TOO!

THEY ALSO LIKE TO DIG HOLES UNDER THE SNOW TO KEEP WARM WHILE THEY SLEEP.
SPEAKING OF SNOWSHOEING, DO YOU KNOW IF WE AVOIDED DRIVING JUST 10 MILES EVERY WEEK, AND WALKED INSTEAD, WE WOULD ELIMINATE 500 POUNDS OF CARBON DIOXIDE FROM ENTERING THE ATMOSPHERE?
REALLY? THAT MUCH?
YOU BET! DRIVING CARS, CUTTING DOWN TREES, AND OPERATING FACTORIES ARE JUST A FEW EXAMPLES OF ACTIVITIES THAT FORCE LARGE AMOUNTS OF CARBON DIOXIDE INTO THE AIR.

IN *1931*, THE STEEL CARGO STEAMER *BAYCHIMO* EXPLORED THE ARCTIC. WHEN THE SHIP BECAME TRAPPED IN THE ICE, THE CREW MOVED ASHORE FOR SAFETY. WHEN THE ICE CLEARED, THE CREW HURRIED BACK ONBOARD AND SET SAIL, BUT ONCE AGAIN, THE ICE GRIPPED THE LITTLE STEAMER. THIS TIME, THE FROZEN SEA DID NOT LET GO, SEALING THE FATE OF THE *BAYCHIMO* FOREVER. ALTHOUGH THE CAPTAIN AND HIS CREW WERE EVENTUALLY RESCUED, THE STEAMER WAS LEFT BEHIND, WHERE—LEGEND HAS IT—IT CONTINUES TO DRIFT AMONG THE ICE BY ITSELF.

HEY, LOOK! LITTLE FLOWERS!
NO WAY!
THEY ARE ARCTIC POPPIES, A SPECIES OF RARE FLOWER FOUND ONLY IN THE ARCTIC.
SINCE IT IS SUMMER, THERE SHOULD BE SOME VEGETATION PEEKING THROUGH HERE AND THERE.
WHAT? THERE ARE BEES UP HERE TOO?
IT'S A BUMBLEBEE!
YES, IT'S AN ARCTIC BUMBLEBEE.
AS YOU KIDS MAY HAVE STUDIED IN SCIENCE CLASS, EVEN IN THESE COLD NORTHERN REGIONS OF THE WORLD, PLANTS NEED POLLINATION TO KEEP REPRODUCING, SO THE ARCTIC BUMBLEBEES, WHICH FABIEN HAS IDENTIFIED, FLY FROM BLOOM TO BLOOM, HELPING THEMSELVES TO NECTAR WHILE NUDGING THE PLANTS ALONG.
BUT IT'S SO COLD. HOW DO THESE BEES SURVIVE?
LIKE ALL COLD-BLOODED CREATURES IN A COLD CLIMATE, ARCTIC BUMBLEBEES MUST GENERATE HEAT ANY WAY THEY CAN. YOU'LL OFTEN FIND THEM RESTING IN THE SUN, BUILDING UP ENOUGH HEAT SO THEY CAN FLY.
WOW, I HAD NO IDEA.
THE MUSCLES OF THE ARCTIC BUMBLEBEE MUST REACH *86°F* BEFORE IT'S WARM ENOUGH TO TAKE FLIGHT.

DAY 2: MARCH 18, 11:04 AM
I'D LIKE FOR ALL OF YOU TO MEET THE NATIVE MEN AND WOMEN OF THIS REGION, KNOWN AS THE "INUIT."
THE INUIT ARE DESCENDANTS OF THE THULE CULTURE, WHO EMERGED FROM WESTERN ALASKA AROUND 1000 C.E. AND SPREAD EASTWARD ACROSS THE ARCTIC. THE PALEO-ESKIMOS, HOWEVER, WERE AMONG THE FIRST PEOPLE TO COLONIZE THE NORTH AMERICAN ARCTIC, LONG BEFORE THE ARRIVAL OF THE ANCESTORS OF MODERN INUIT.

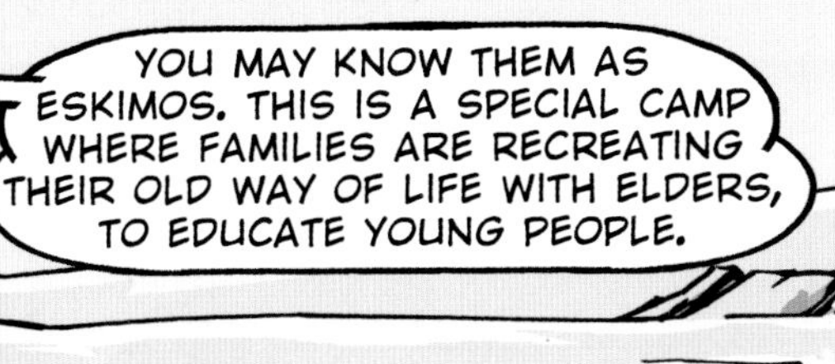
YOU MAY KNOW THEM AS ESKIMOS. THIS IS A SPECIAL CAMP WHERE FAMILIES ARE RECREATING THEIR OLD WAY OF LIFE WITH ELDERS, TO EDUCATE YOUNG PEOPLE.
PEOPLE HAVE INHABITED VARIOUS REGIONS OF THE ARCTIC FOR THOUSANDS OF YEARS. THE EARLIEST KNOWN EVIDENCE OF HUMANS IN THE ARCTIC IS 40,000 YEARS AGO IN WESTERN SIBERIA.
COMMON INUIT WORDS
ULAAKUT GOOD MORNING
ULUUKUUT GOOD AFTERNOON
QANUIIPIT HOW ARE YOU?
QANUINGITUNGA I'M FINE
QUJANAAMIIK THANK YOU
ILAALI YOU'RE WELCOME

I'M HOPING THE INUIT CAN PROVIDE US WITH A CLUE ON WHERE TO FIND A DUMBO OCTOPUS.

WHY DO THEY HANG THEIR CLOTHES OUTSIDE?

SO THEY CAN DRY THEM.

SPEAKING OF WHICH, I LIKE TO WASH MY CLOTHES IN COLD WATER AND AIR-DRY THEM. SOMETHING ABOUT THAT FRESH CRISP AIR...

IF WE DID THAT FOR JUST 6 MONTHS, WE'D ELIMINATE MORE THAN 1,000 POUNDS OF CARBON DIOXIDE FROM ENTERING OUR ATMOSPHERE.

THAT'S A LOT FOR DOING SO LITTLE!

THE INUIT'S DIETARY STAPLE IS SEA MAMMALS, SUCH AS SEALS, WHALES, AND WALRUS. THEY ALSO EAT FISH, ESPECIALLY ARCTIC COD, A SMALL SILVER FISH, ALSO KNOWN AS POLAR COD. THIS SPECIES SWIMS UNDER THE ICE AND FEEDS ON CRABS AND SMALLER FISH.

IT'S REALLY COZY IN HERE.

AND QUITE WARM... AND THEY DON'T EVEN HAVE A HEATER. I BET THAT SAVES ON CARBON DIOXIDE TOO.

NOW YOU'RE LEARNING, ROCCO. WE CAN ELIMINATE 2,000 POUNDS OF CARBON DIOXIDE FROM ENTERING THE ATMOSPHERE EVERY YEAR IF WE LOWER OUR THERMOSTAT ONLY 2 DEGREES IN THE WINTER AND RAISE IT 2 DEGREES IN THE SUMMER.

MY PARENTS AND I WILL DEFINITELY DO THAT WHEN I GET HOME.

YOU HAVE COME A LONG WAY, MY FRIENDS.
YES, WE HAVE, AND WE'RE HONORED TO BE HERE.
AND WHAT ARE YOU IN SEARCH OF THIS TIME, FABIEN?

WE ARE LOOKING FOR A DUMBO OCTOPUS, A VERY RARE ANIMAL THAT LIVES DEEP UNDER THE ICE.
INTERESTING YOU SAY THAT.
LAST NIGHT IN MY DREAM, I SAW A BRIGHT LIGHT.

I WENT OUTSIDE AND LOOKED INTO THE HEAVENS, AND THERE, IN THE SKY, A GREAT OCTOPUS APPEARED.
ONE OF ITS ARMS POINTED AT ME, THEN TO THE ICE BELOW THE CONSTELLATION URSA MAJOR— "GREAT BEAR."
IN THE MORNING, I SHARED MY STORY WITH MY BROTHERS AND THEY TOLD ME ABOUT A LARGE CAVE AT THE BOTTOM OF THE SEA.
IF YOU FIND THIS CAVE, YOU MAY FIND YOUR DUMBO OCTOPUS.
THANK YOU FOR SHARING WITH US YOUR INCREDIBLE DREAM.
QUJANAAMIIK!
AHHH...I SEE YOU'RE LEARNING YOUR INUIT. VERY GOOD, MY YOUNG FRIEND.

STEP 1: LOCATION

CHOOSE AN AREA WITH HARD, COMPACT SNOW. USING THE SNOW SPADE, MAKE A CIRCLE IN THE SNOW ABOUT THE SIZE OF THE HOUSE YOU WANT TO BUILD, BUT DON'T MAKE IT TOO BIG.

STEP 2: THE BLOCKS

USING THE SNOW SAW, CUT LARGE BLOCKS OUT OF THE SNOW FOR THE BASE OF THE DOME. CUT SMALLER BLOCKS FOR THE TOP. SMOOTH THE EDGES OF EACH BLOCK WITH THE SNOW KNIFE.

STEP 3: BUILDING

STACK THE LARGE BLOCKS TIGHTLY, SIDE BY SIDE, AROUND THE OUTER CIRCLE YOU DREW IN THE SNOW. SLANT THE BLOCKS INWARD—OTHERWISE YOU WILL BE BUILDING A TOWER. FOR THE ENTRANCE, PLACE FOUR BLOCKS POINTING OUTWARD, TWO ON EACH SIDE. USE MORE BLOCKS TO MAKE A SMALL ROOF ON THE ENTRANCE. NOW KEEP ADDING THE BLOCKS TO FILL IN THE CIRCLE, LEAVING AN OPENING TO THE ENTRANCE. MAKE SURE TO REMOVE ALL THE SNOW THAT IS PILING UP INSIDE. THE FINAL BLOCKS CAN BE BROUGHT IN THROUGH THE ENTRANCE AND STACKED FROM INSIDE THE SNOW HOUSE.

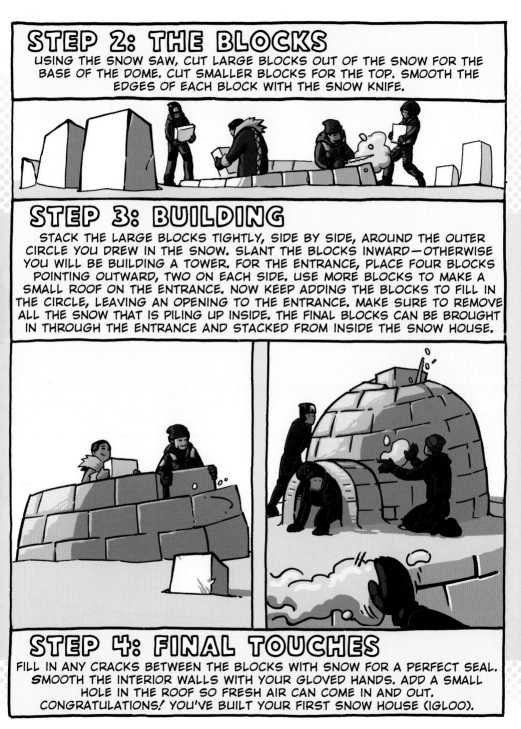

STEP 4: FINAL TOUCHES

FILL IN ANY CRACKS BETWEEN THE BLOCKS WITH SNOW FOR A PERFECT SEAL. SMOOTH THE INTERIOR WALLS WITH YOUR GLOVED HANDS. ADD A SMALL HOLE IN THE ROOF SO FRESH AIR CAN COME IN AND OUT. CONGRATULATIONS! YOU'VE BUILT YOUR FIRST SNOW HOUSE (IGLOO).

DAY 3: MARCH 19, 5:30 AM

STERN OBSERVATORY

IF WHAT THE INUIT SAY IS TRUE, AND IF OUR CALCULATIONS ARE CORRECT, OUR POINT OF ENTRY SHOULD BE RIGHT WHERE THE X IS ON THIS MAP.

LOOK OVER THERE! THERE'S AN OPENING IN THE ICE.

WE'LL HAVE TO NAVIGATE OUR DEEP-SEA SUBMERSIBLE THROUGH THE NARROW CRACKS IN THE ICE UNTIL WE CAN REACH THE PLOTTED ENTRY POINT. FROM THERE, WE'LL DROP TO THE BOTTOM AND HOPEFULLY FIND OUR CAVE...

...AND OUR OCTOPUS?
AND OUR OCTOPUS.

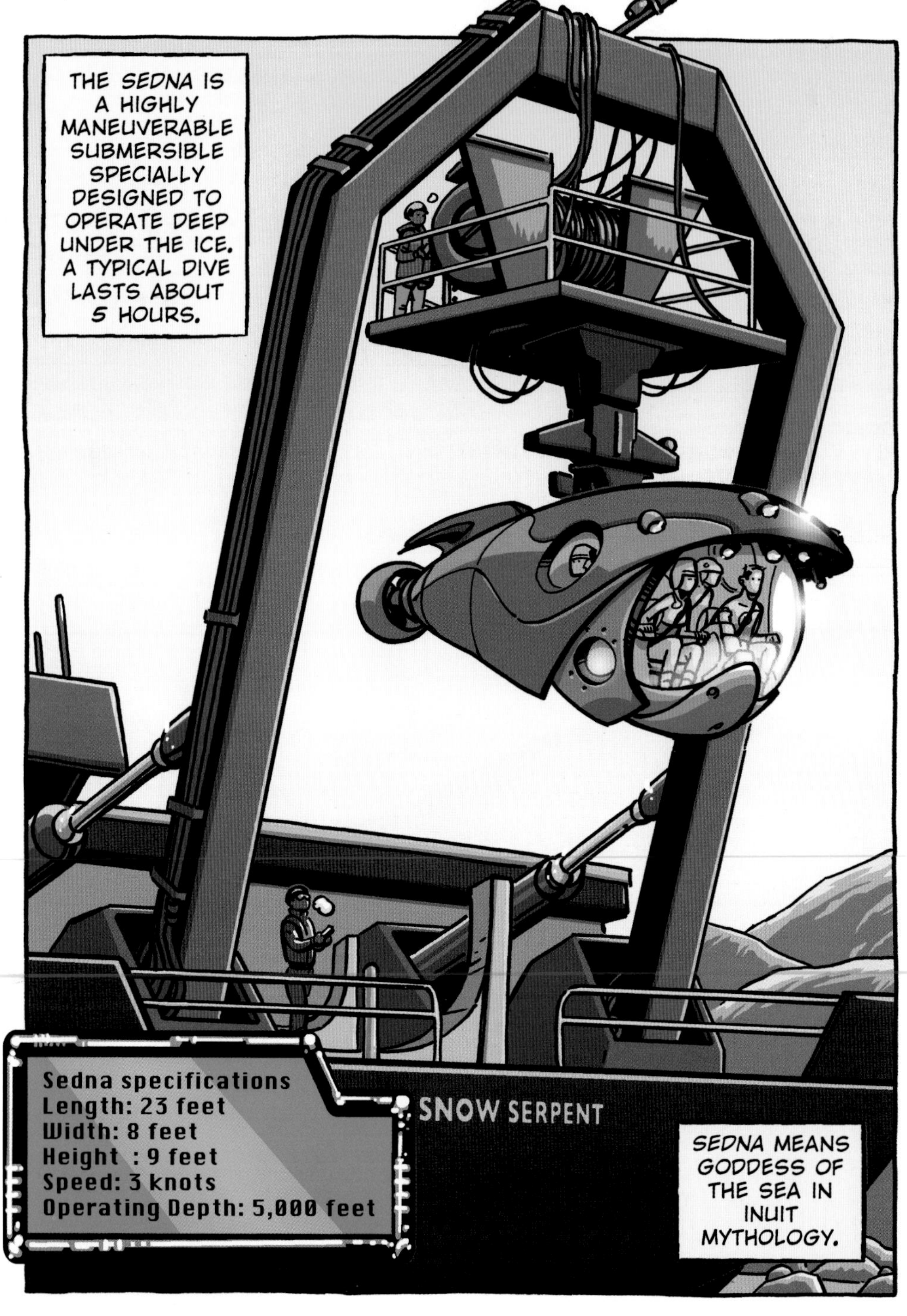
THE *SEDNA* IS A HIGHLY MANEUVERABLE SUBMERSIBLE SPECIALLY DESIGNED TO OPERATE DEEP UNDER THE ICE. A TYPICAL DIVE LASTS ABOUT 5 HOURS.
Sedna specifications
Length: 23 feet
Width: 8 feet
Height : 9 feet
Speed: 3 knots
Operating Depth: 5,000 feet
SNOW SERPENT
SEDNA MEANS GODDESS OF THE SEA IN INUIT MYTHOLOGY.

AS YOU CAN SEE, IT TAKES A CREW TO LAUNCH US INTO THE CHANNEL. THE FIRST IS THE CRANE OPERATOR, WHO JUST LIFTED THE *SEDNA* FROM THE DECK AND GENTLY PLACED HER IN THE WATER. THE SUBMERSIBLE SUPERVISOR OVERSEES THE PROCESS, ALONG WITH THE SUB OPERATIONS COORDINATOR. ANOTHER CREW MEMBER IS IN CHARGE OF HANDLING THE CRANE LINES TO MAKE SURE NOTHING GETS TANGLED UP.

WHAT ABOUT OUR CAPTAIN?

HE'LL BE WITH THE SUB OPERATIONS COORDINATOR UP IN THE BRIDGE AND WILL BE IN CONSTANT CONTACT WITH US THROUGH OUR HEADSETS WHILE WE ARE BELOW.

!
THE BELUGA WHALE IS A SMALL TOOTHED WHALE THAT IS BRIGHT WHITE. UNLIKE OTHER WHALES, THE BELUGA'S NECK IS FLEXIBLE, ALLOWING THE MAMMAL TO TURN ITS HEAD TO LOOK FOR FISH. THE WHALE ALSO HAS NO DORSAL FIN, WHICH MAKES SWIMMING UNDER THE ICE MUCH EASIER. BELUGAS FEED ON VARIOUS FISH AND SQUID AND CAN DIVE TO DEPTHS OF 3,000 FEET.

LOOK AT ALL THE SCARS ON THE WHALES. HAVE THEY BEEN FIGHTING?
THEY'RE ACTUALLY PAW AND TEETH MARKS FROM POLAR BEARS.
NO WAY!
BELUGA MEANS "WHITE ONE" IN RUSSIAN.

ALTHOUGH THESE BELUGAS ARE BETWEEN 12 AND 14 FEET AND WEIGH ABOUT 2,000 POUNDS, AN ADULT POLAR BEAR CAN PULL A BELUGA OUT OF THE WATER IF GIVEN THE CHANCE.
THE BEARS AREN'T ALWAYS SUCCESSFUL THOUGH, WHICH EXPLAINS THE BELUGAS' SCARRED BODIES.

POLAR BEARS MOVING IN FAST!
POLAR BEAR Stats
Height: 8 to 10 feet
Weight: Adult males: 500 to 1,700 pounds
Adult females: 200 to 700 pounds
Life Span: 20 to 25 years
WE SEE 'EM, CAP.

POLAR BEARS ARE AMONG THE LARGEST PREDATORS IN THE WORLD, AND THEY'RE ONLY FOUND IN THE ARCTIC.
THEY ALSO HAVE AN INCREDIBLE SENSE OF SMELL.
THEY MUST BE AFTER THE WHALES...
I'M SURE THEY ARE.
POLAR BEARS ARE EXCELLENT SWIMMERS AND HAVE A THICK LAYER OF FAT THAT ALLOWS THEM TO FLOAT EASILY IN THE WATER.

THEY SURE LOOK HUNGRY.
YES, THEY DO.
DOESN'T LOOK LIKE THEY'VE HAD MUCH TO EAT LATELY. MOST OF THE TIME THEY FEED ON SEALS, BUT IT APPEARS THESE TWO ARE AFTER LARGER PREY.
THE POLAR BEAR'S FUR IS ACTUALLY MADE OF CLEAR, COLORLESS HAIRS. THE HAIRS SCATTER LIGHT, MAKING IT APPEAR WHITE (OR SOMETIMES YELLOW, DEPENDING UPON THE ANGLE OF THE SUN).

DON'T THEIR FEET GET COLD IN ALL OF THIS SNOW AND ICE?
YOU WOULD THINK, BUT THE POLAR BEARS' FUR IS MUCH THICKER THAN OTHER BEARS', AND THEY HAVE HAIR THAT COVERS THE TOPS OF THEIR TOES FOR ADDED WARMTH.
JUST LIKE WE'RE STAYING NICE AND TOASTY THANKS TO OUR FULLY INSULATED AND HEATED SUBZERO CLOTHING, POLAR BEARS HAVE A 6-INCH LAYER OF FAT THAT INSULATES THEM FROM THE EXTREME COLD OF THE ARCTIC.
AND THEIR SKIN IS BLACK, WHICH HELPS THE BEARS ABSORB HEAT FROM THE SUN.

WHAT'S THAT SMALL ANIMAL FOLLOWING THE BEARS?
THAT'S AN ARCTIC FOX, WHICH IS WELL CAMOUFLAGED TO HELP IT HUNT.
ALTHOUGH THIS FOX SEEMS TO BE LOOKING FOR AN EASY MEAL.
FOR SURE. OFTEN ARCTIC FOXES WILL FOLLOW POLAR BEARS IN HOPES OF FEEDING ON THEIR LEFTOVERS.
THE ARCTIC FOX HAS ONE OF THE WARMEST FURS OF ANY MAMMAL, EVEN WARMER THAN THE POLAR BEAR.
FABIEN, I'M NOT LIKING WHAT I'M SEEING.
I AGREE, CAPTAIN. LET'S ABORT THE DIVE UNTIL THE ANIMALS LEAVE THE AREA. THERE ISN'T ROOM FOR ALL OF US IN THIS NARROW CHANNEL.

DAY 4: MARCH 20, 8:46 AM
I SEE WE HAVE SOME NEW FRIENDS THIS MORNING.

OLIVIA AND ROCCO, DO YOU KNOW WALRUS ARE THE LARGEST PINNIPEDS IN THE ARCTIC? THEY ALSO HAVE ENORMOUS TUSKS, WHICH ARE ACTUALLY THEIR CANINE TEETH. THE TUSKS ARE MADE OF IVORY AND GROW TO BE 2 FEET LONG IN FEMALES AND 4 FEET LONG IN MALES.

PINNIPEDS: "PINNI" MEANS "WING" OR "FIN," AND "PEDIS" MEANS "FOOT." SEALS AND SEA LIONS ARE ALSO PINNIPEDS.

I THINK WALRUS ARE SUCH COOL MAMMALS.
I AGREE.

THE SCIENTIFIC NAME FOR WALRUS IS *ODOBENUS ROSMARUS*, WHICH MEANS "TOOTH WALKER."

WHEN SEARCHING FOR FOOD, WALRUS CAN DIVE TO INCREDIBLE DEPTHS AND STAY UNDERWATER FOR ALMOST 30 MINUTES.
THAT'S A LONG TIME.

THE LARGER SEALS ARE THE HOODED SEALS, NAMED BECAUSE OF THEIR LARGE NASAL CAVITY, OR "HOOD." THEY ARE A FAVORITE PREY FOR POLAR BEARS AND KILLER WHALES. THERE ARE ALSO HARP SEALS, WHICH ARE BORN WHITE AND FLUFFY TO BLEND IN WITH THE SNOW, PROTECTING THEM FROM PREDATORS.

WHAT DO THEY EAT?
PRIMARILY CLAMS. THAT'S A FAVORITE FOOD OF THEIRS.
IF YOU LOOK JUST BEYOND THE WALRUS, YOU'LL SEE HARP SEALS, HOODED SEALS, AND RINGED SEALS.
WHICH ARE WHICH?

BUT THE MASTERS AT AVOIDING CAPTURE ARE THE RINGED SEALS, EASILY IDENTIFIED BY THE DARK SPOTS AND LIGHT GRAY RINGS ON THEIR FUR. THEY WILL BURY THEMSELVES BENEATH THE SNOW. WHEN A PREDATOR LIKE A POLAR BEAR APPROACHES, THE RINGED SEALS FOLLOW AN ESCAPE TUNNEL THAT LEADS THEM UNDERWATER AND AWAY FROM DANGER.

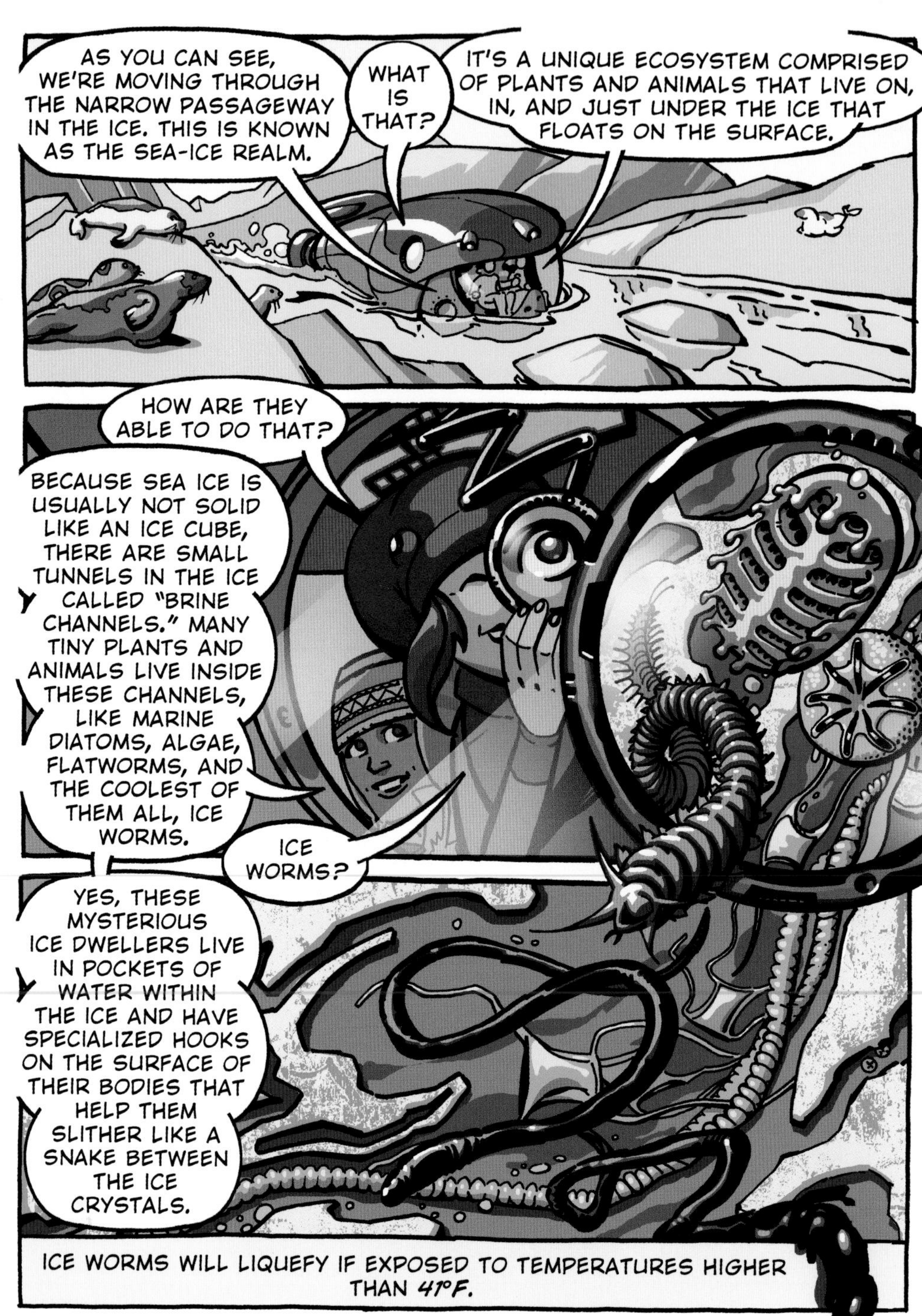
AS YOU CAN SEE, WE'RE MOVING THROUGH THE NARROW PASSAGEWAY IN THE ICE. THIS IS KNOWN AS THE SEA-ICE REALM.
WHAT IS THAT?
IT'S A UNIQUE ECOSYSTEM COMPRISED OF PLANTS AND ANIMALS THAT LIVE ON, IN, AND JUST UNDER THE ICE THAT FLOATS ON THE SURFACE.
HOW ARE THEY ABLE TO DO THAT?
BECAUSE SEA ICE IS USUALLY NOT SOLID LIKE AN ICE CUBE, THERE ARE SMALL TUNNELS IN THE ICE CALLED "BRINE CHANNELS." MANY TINY PLANTS AND ANIMALS LIVE INSIDE THESE CHANNELS, LIKE MARINE DIATOMS, ALGAE, FLATWORMS, AND THE COOLEST OF THEM ALL, ICE WORMS.
ICE WORMS?
YES, THESE MYSTERIOUS ICE DWELLERS LIVE IN POCKETS OF WATER WITHIN THE ICE AND HAVE SPECIALIZED HOOKS ON THE SURFACE OF THEIR BODIES THAT HELP THEM SLITHER LIKE A SNAKE BETWEEN THE ICE CRYSTALS.
ICE WORMS WILL LIQUEFY IF EXPOSED TO TEMPERATURES HIGHER THAN 41°F.

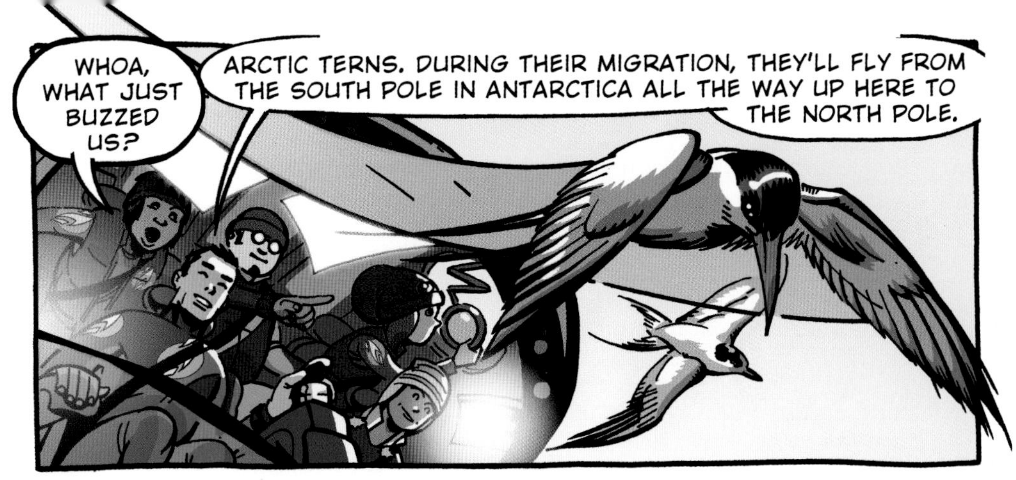

HOW LONG A FLIGHT IS THAT?

MORE THAN *44,000* MILES!

WHICH MAKES THE ARCTIC TERN'S MIGRATION THE LONGEST ON THE PLANET!

THE ARCTIC TERN'S MIGRATION IS SO LONG THAT THE BIRD SEES TWO SUMMERS EACH YEAR.

OH NO! WE HAVE A VERY UPSET BOWHEAD WHALE THAT HAS SOMEHOW TRAPPED ITSELF IN THE ICE.
IT'S HUGE!
BOWHEAD WHALES EAT LARGE AMOUNTS OF PLANKTON AND TINY SHRIMP CALLED "KRILL" BY CONSTANTLY SWIMMING WITH THEIR MOUTHS OPEN. LIKE ALL TOOTHLESS WHALES, THE BOWHEAD FILTERS ITS FOOD USING BALEEN, WHICH ARE FLAT, FLEXIBLE PLATES THAT HELP SEPARATE THE FOOD FROM THE WATER. BOWHEADS ALSO BREATHE AIR AT THE SURFACE LIKE OTHER WHALES, BUT THEY DO SO THROUGH TWO BLOWHOLES INSTEAD OF THE USUAL ONE, RESULTING IN A 20-FOOT SPOUT OF MISTY AIR.

THIS WHALE'S LARGE BOW-SHAPED HEAD ACCOUNTS FOR ALMOST HALF OF ITS 50-FOOT LENGTH.
THAT'S RIGHT, AND ALTHOUGH IT HAS VERY SMALL EYES, I'M SURE IT KNOWS WE'RE HERE. ONE SLAP OF ITS TAIL AND OUR MISSION WILL BE OVER IN A HURRY.

WHALES LIKE THE BOWHEAD THRIVE IN THE ARCTIC. HUMPBACKS, BLUES, MINKE, FIN, AND GRAY WHALES ALSO MAKE THE ANNUAL TRIP TO THE NORTH POLE. IN FACT, GRAY WHALES MIGRATE *12,500* MILES FROM THE ARCTIC TO MEXICO AND BACK EVERY YEAR.

BLUE

FIN

HUMPBACK

GRAY

MINKE

AH, GUYS...? WE HAVE ANOTHER PROBLEM!

THE WHALE'S TALL GEYSER-LIKE SPOUT IS DRAWING ATTENTION, AND THOSE HUNGRY BEARS HAVE PICKED UP ON IT.

THEY'RE SURE IN A HURRY THIS TIME.
THEY MUST BE REALLY HUNGRY.

I SUGGEST WE ABORT AGAIN.
WE CAN'T. THE NARROW CHANNEL WE JUST NAVIGATED IS NOW COMPLETELY SEALED UP. WE'RE TRAPPED IN HERE WITH THE WHALE.

WHY IS THE WHALE SPOUTING SO MUCH?

THAT MEANS IT'S GETTING READY TO DIVE... FABIEN, WE NEED TO GIVE THIS WHALE SOME ROOM.

IS IT ME, OR IS THE OPENING WE'RE IN GETTING SMALLER?

THE ICE IS SHIFTING AND YES, IT'S GETTING SMALLER.

WE'RE RUNNING OUT OF ROOM!

Ballast Tank

Thrusters

THE *SEDNA* MOVES USING SIX THRUSTERS: THREE THAT PROPEL THE SUB FORWARD AND BACKWARD, TWO FOR UP AND DOWN, AND ONE FOR TURNING. DIVING TO THE SEA BOTTOM IS PERFORMED BY FILLING THE SUB'S BALLAST TANKS WITH WATER, WHICH OLIVIA JUST ACCOMPLISHED BY FLIPPING THE FOUR SWITCHES.

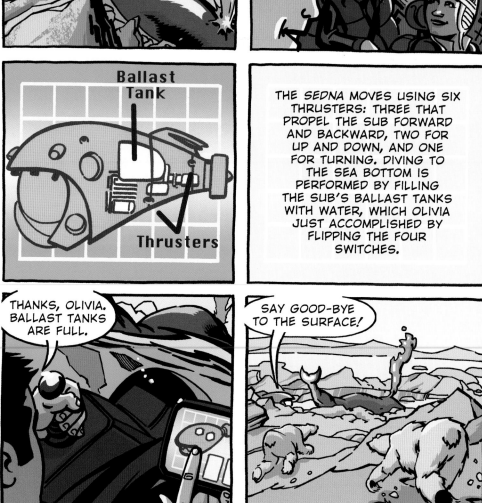

TOPSIDE, THIS IS THE SEDNA. DO YOU COPY?

WE COPY YOU LOUD AND CLEAR.

WE ARE BEGINNING OUR DESCENT IN THREE...
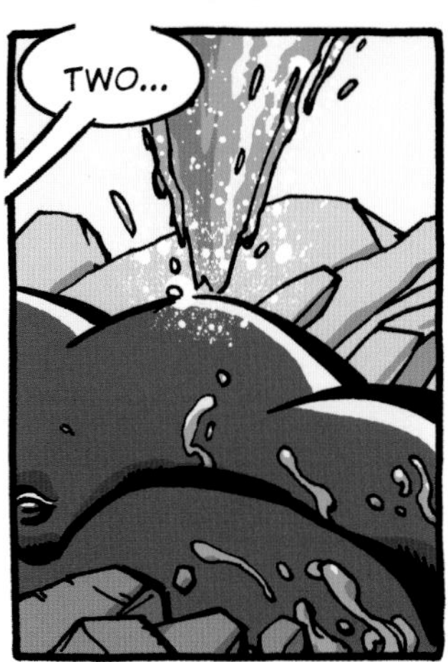
TWO...

ONE... VENTING!

GO, GO, GO!

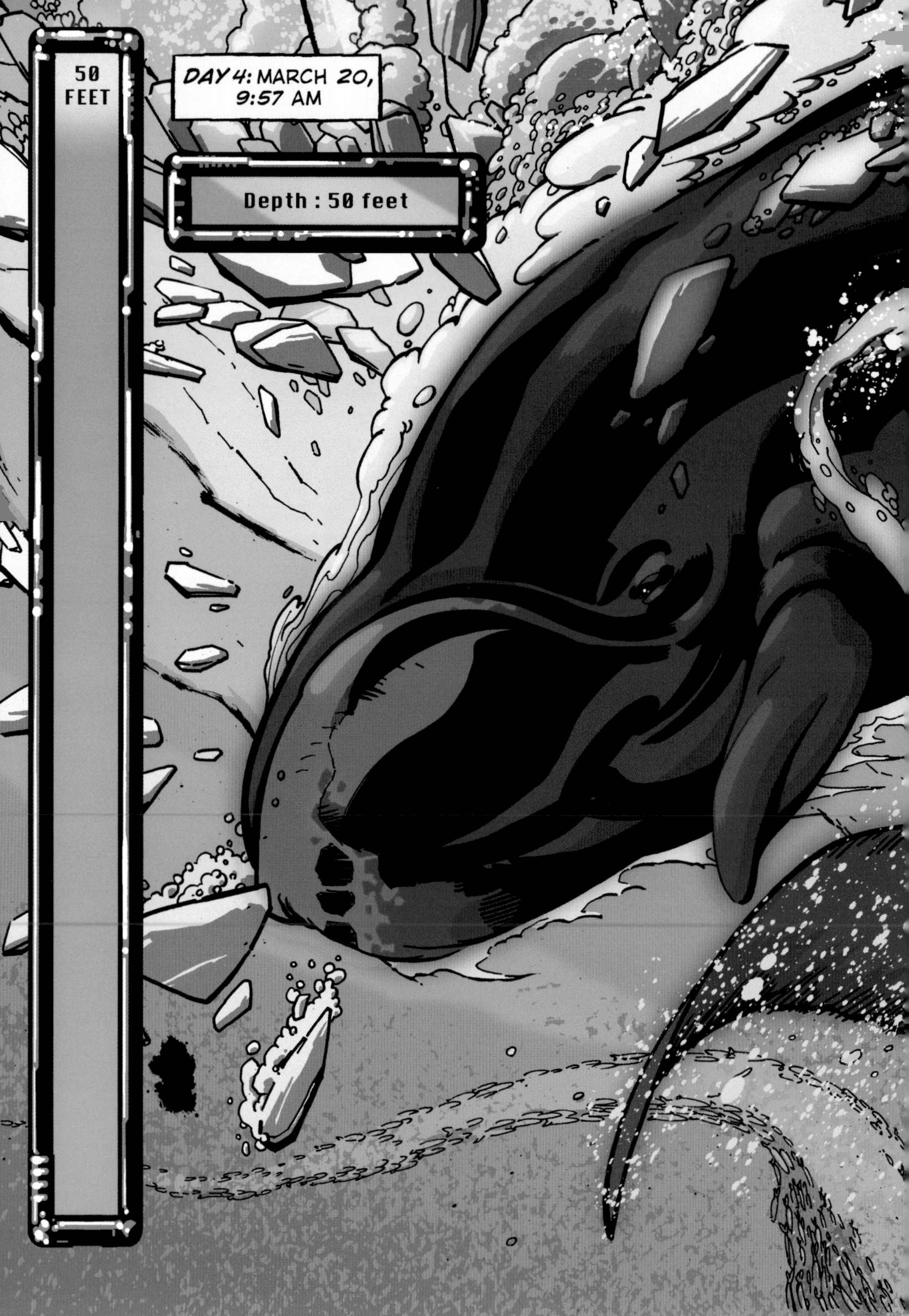
50 FEET
DAY 4: MARCH 20, 9:57 AM
Depth : 50 feet

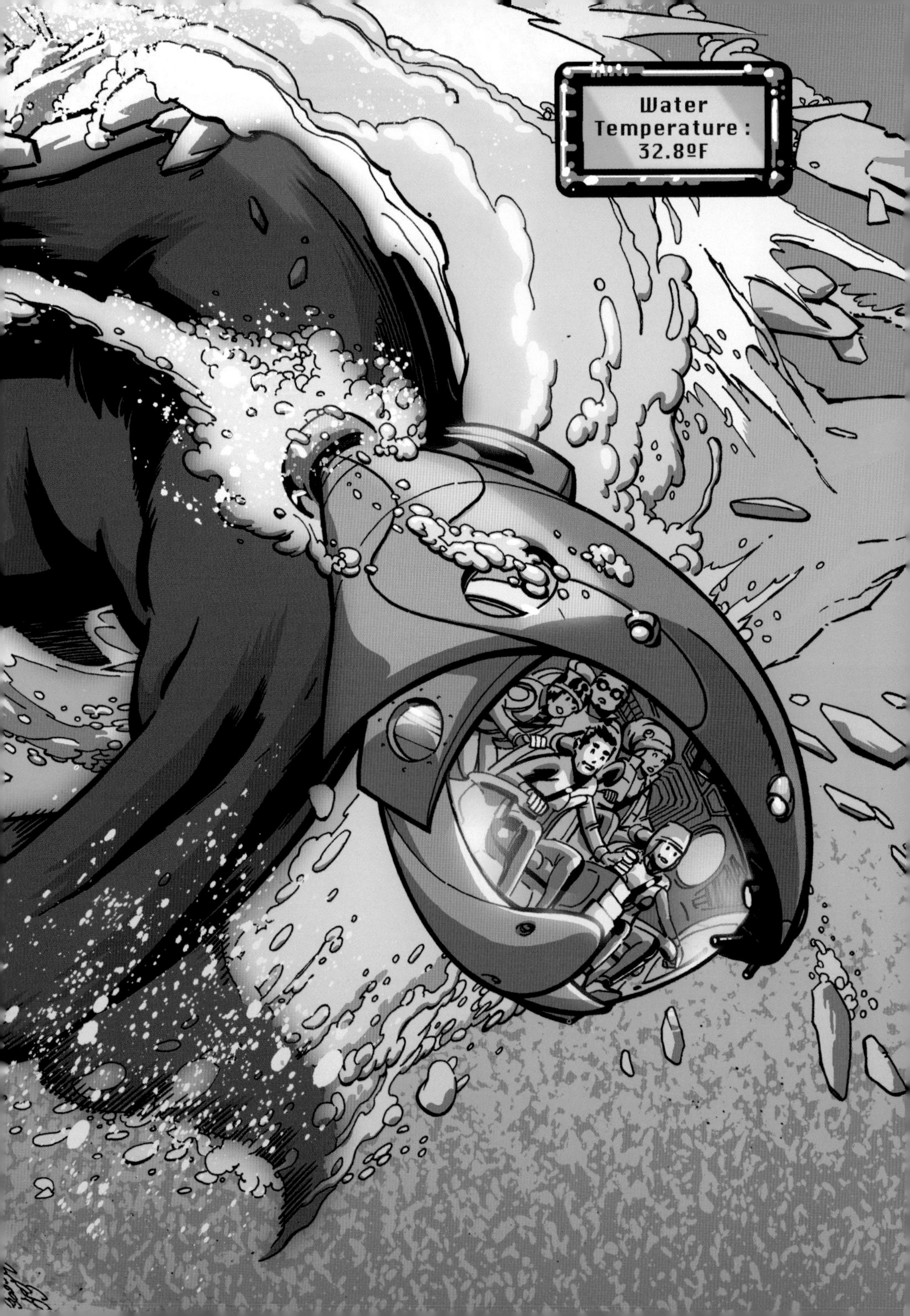
Water
Temperature :
32.8ºF

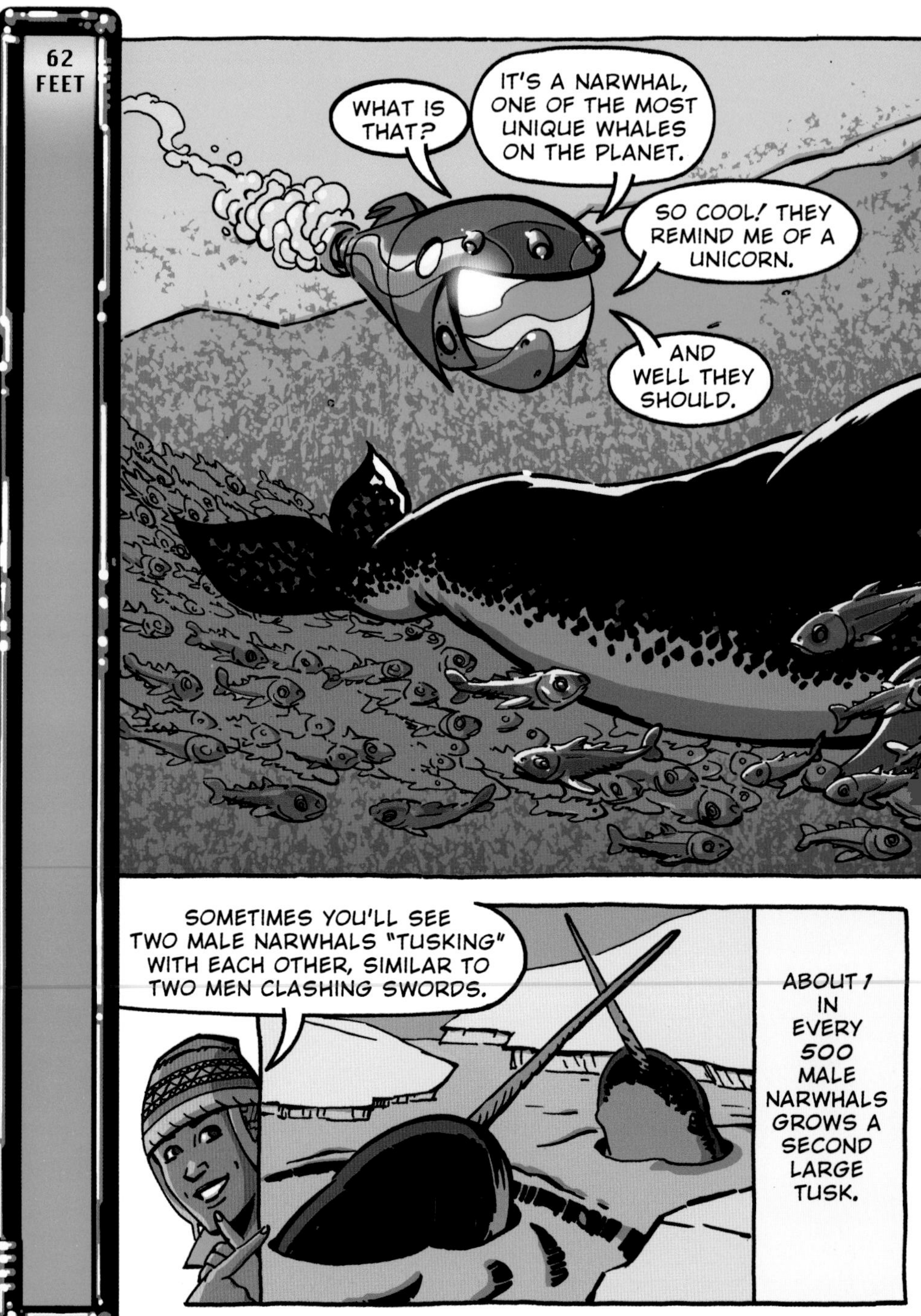
62 FEET
WHAT IS THAT?
IT'S A NARWHAL, ONE OF THE MOST UNIQUE WHALES ON THE PLANET.
SO COOL! THEY REMIND ME OF A UNICORN.
AND WELL THEY SHOULD.
SOMETIMES YOU'LL SEE TWO MALE NARWHALS "TUSKING" WITH EACH OTHER, SIMILAR TO TWO MEN CLASHING SWORDS.
ABOUT 1 IN EVERY 500 MALE NARWHALS GROWS A SECOND LARGE TUSK.

THEIR LONG SPIRALING TUSK IS ACTUALLY A TOOTH THAT GROWS TO 9 FEET LONG.

THAT SPIRAL TOOTH ALSO CONTAINS MORE THAN 10 MILLION NERVES, WHICH ALLOW NARWHALS TO DETECT CHANGES IN WATER TEMPERATURE.

WHAT THE HECK IS THAT BIZARRE-LOOKING CREATURE NEXT TO THE GLASS?

130 FEET
CHECK OUT THAT JELLYFISH. IT'S SO COOL-LOOKING!
IT IS, INDEED.
THAT GIANT JELLY IS A LION'S MANE JELLYFISH. IT IS THE LARGEST KNOWN SPECIES OF JELLYFISH, CAPABLE OF GROWING UP TO 120 FEET LONG.
IT EARNED ITS NAME FROM ITS RED AND YELLOW TENTACLES, WHICH RESEMBLE THE COLOR OF A LION'S MANE.

350 FEET
OH MY GOSH!
DON'T BE ALARMED. THE KILLER WHALE WON'T ATTACK...
...AT LEAST NOT US.
GLORIA'S RIGHT. THESE TOOTHED WHALES, ALSO KNOWN AS ORCAS, PREFER FISH, OCTOPI, SQUID, SHARKS, SEALS, AND EVEN BIRDS.
THEY'VE ALSO BEEN KNOWN TO PURSUE OTHER WHALES.
THANK YOU. THAT IS REASSURING.

360 FEET

KILLER WHALES ARE THE LARGEST MEMBER OF THE DOLPHIN FAMILY AND FEMALES CAN LIVE UP TO 50 YEARS IN THE WILD.

KILLER WHALES ARE ALSO VERY STRONG SWIMMERS AND, LIKE NARWHALS, OFTEN TRAVEL IN GROUPS CALLED PODS. PODS USUALLY CONSIST OF 5 TO 30 WHALES, ALTHOUGH SOME PODS MAY BE AS LARGE AS 100 OR MORE. THIS ONE MUST HAVE LEFT THE POD TO CHECK US OUT.

A MALE KILLER WHALE CAN GROW TO 23 FEET LONG AND WEIGH 7 TO 10 TONS. FEMALES CAN REACH 21 FEET AND WEIGH 4 TO 6 TONS.

1000 FEET

DAY 4: MARCH 20, 10:40 AM

WHOA, 1,000 FEET!

1,000 FEET AND COUNTING...

BY THE WAY, IF YOU KIDS ARE STILL LOOKING FOR WAYS TO ELIMINATE CARBON DIOXIDE, CONSIDER USING LESS HOT WATER AT HOME, SINCE IT TAKES A LOT OF ENERGY TO HEAT WATER. JUST A LITTLE LESS HOT WATER IN YOUR SHOWER WILL REMOVE 350 POUNDS OF CARBON DIOXIDE FROM ENTERING THE ATMOSPHERE EVERY YEAR.

SEDNA, THIS IS TOPSIDE. HOW ARE YOU FARING DOWN THERE?
DOING WELL. WE'RE AT 1,000 FEET AND STILL DESCENDING.

1220 FEET
WE'RE PASSING THROUGH THE ARCTIC OCEAN'S DEEP-WATER REGION, KNOWN AS THE PELAGIC REALM.
THE PELAGIC REALM INCLUDES ORGANISMS THAT LIVE IN THE WATER COLUMN BETWEEN THE OCEAN SURFACE AND THE BOTTOM.
I THINK IT'S TIME FOR SOME LIGHT DOWN HERE.
AGREED. OLIVIA, THERE'S A METER PANEL NEXT TO THE PILOT PANEL JUST OVER MY LEFT SHOULDER. DO ME A FAVOR, PLEASE, AND FLIP THE FOUR MIDDLE SWITCHES TO THE ON POSITION.
THAT'S MUCH BETTER, THANK YOU. NOW WE CAN OBSERVE WHAT LIVES DOWN HERE AT THE 1,000 FEET LEVEL.
AND BY USING ONLY THE FORWARD LIGHTS, WE'LL CONSERVE BATTERY POWER DURING OUR DESCENT.

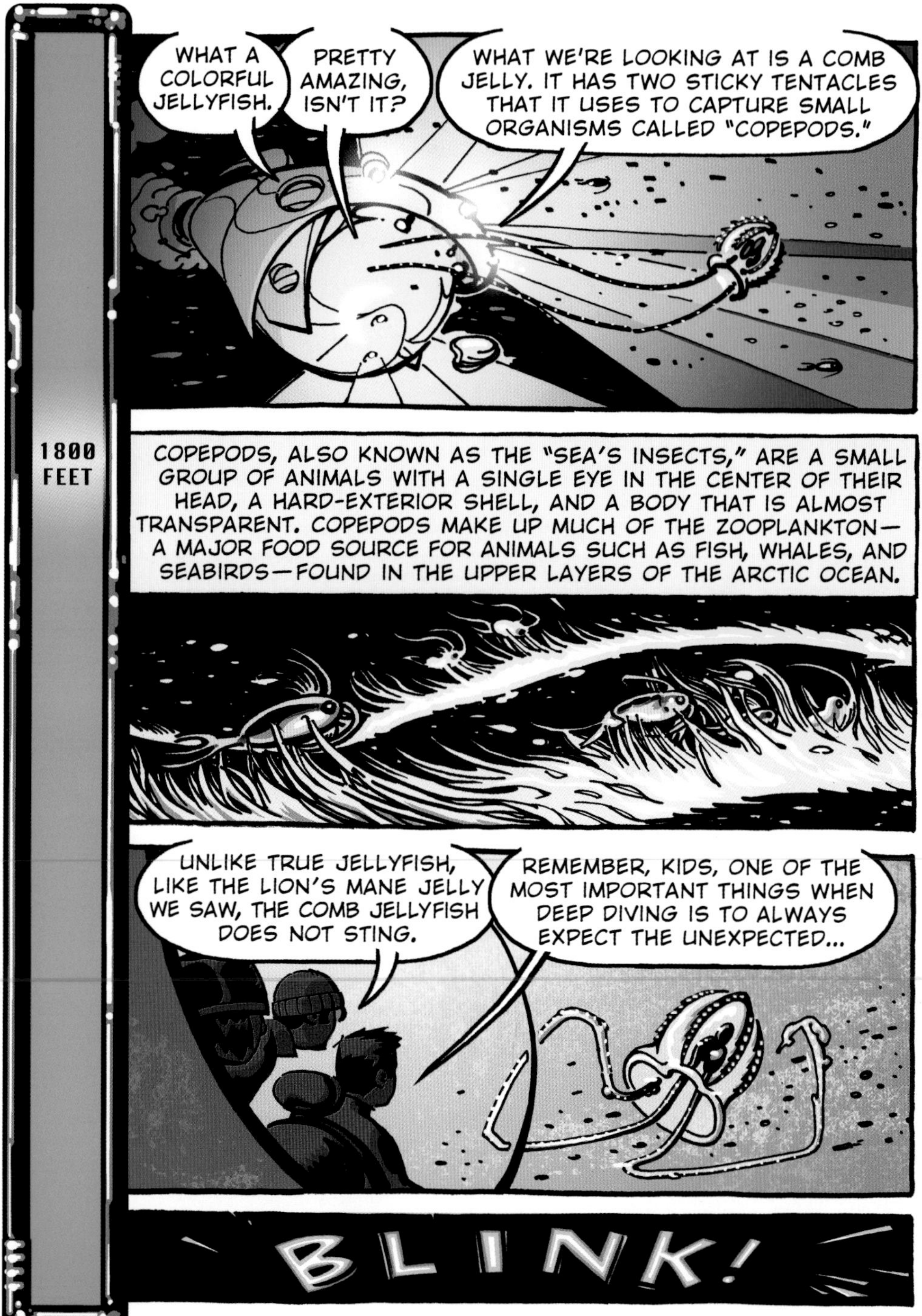

WHAT A COLORFUL JELLYFISH.

PRETTY AMAZING, ISN'T IT?

WHAT WE'RE LOOKING AT IS A COMB JELLY. IT HAS TWO STICKY TENTACLES THAT IT USES TO CAPTURE SMALL ORGANISMS CALLED "COPEPODS."

1800 FEET

COPEPODS, ALSO KNOWN AS THE "SEA'S INSECTS," ARE A SMALL GROUP OF ANIMALS WITH A SINGLE EYE IN THE CENTER OF THEIR HEAD, A HARD-EXTERIOR SHELL, AND A BODY THAT IS ALMOST TRANSPARENT. COPEPODS MAKE UP MUCH OF THE ZOOPLANKTON—A MAJOR FOOD SOURCE FOR ANIMALS SUCH AS FISH, WHALES, AND SEABIRDS—FOUND IN THE UPPER LAYERS OF THE ARCTIC OCEAN.

UNLIKE TRUE JELLYFISH, LIKE THE LION'S MANE JELLY WE SAW, THE COMB JELLYFISH DOES NOT STING.

REMEMBER, KIDS, ONE OF THE MOST IMPORTANT THINGS WHEN DEEP DIVING IS TO ALWAYS EXPECT THE UNEXPECTED...

3500 FEET
DAY 4: MARCH 20, 11:04 AM
TOPSIDE, THIS IS THE SEDNA. BE ADVISED WE ARE AT 3,500 FEET AND HAVE JUST LOST OUR LIGHTS.
COPY THAT. OUR ELECTRONICS LOOK GOOD FROM UP HERE. MUST BE A LOOSE CONNECTION ON YOUR END. ANY CHANCE YOU CAN TROUBLE-SHOOT?
WE'LL GIVE IT A TRY.
HEY, KIDS, IMAGINE LIVING IN COMPLETE DARKNESS LIKE THIS.
MOST OF THE ANIMALS THIS DEEP HAVE NEVER SEEN DAYLIGHT. MANY SPECIES ORIGINATED BEFORE THE DINOSAURS.
YIKES! WHAT ARE THOSE GIANT GLOW-IN-THE-DARK EYES STARING AT US?
WHERE?
OFF TO YOUR RIGHT!
NOT SURE, OLIVIA.
OLIVIA. WE NEED YOUR HELP AGAIN. THERE'S A CIRCUIT BREAKER NEXT TO THE PANEL WHERE YOU TURNED ON THE FORWARD LIGHTS. I NEED YOU TO PLEASE OPEN THAT BOX.
CLICK

OKAY, FABIEN. I HAVE IT OPENED.

GREAT, THANK YOU! NOW LOCATE THE LARGE RED SWITCH THAT SHOULD BE LABELED "MASTER CONTROL SWITCH."

I DON'T SEE IT.

RIGHT THERE, OLIVIA. IN THE LEFT CORNER.

THANKS, ROCCO... I SEE IT, FABIEN.
MASTER CONTROL SWITCH

OKAY, TURN THAT SWITCH TO OFF, GIVE IT ONE SECOND, THEN FLIP IT BACK TO THE ON POSITION.

3500 FEET

WHAT WILL THAT DO?

IT SHOULD RESET THE MAXIMUM ELECTRICAL FLOW WITH MINIMAL LOSS.

HE MEANS RESETTING THAT SWITCH SHOULD GIVE US LIGHT AGAIN.

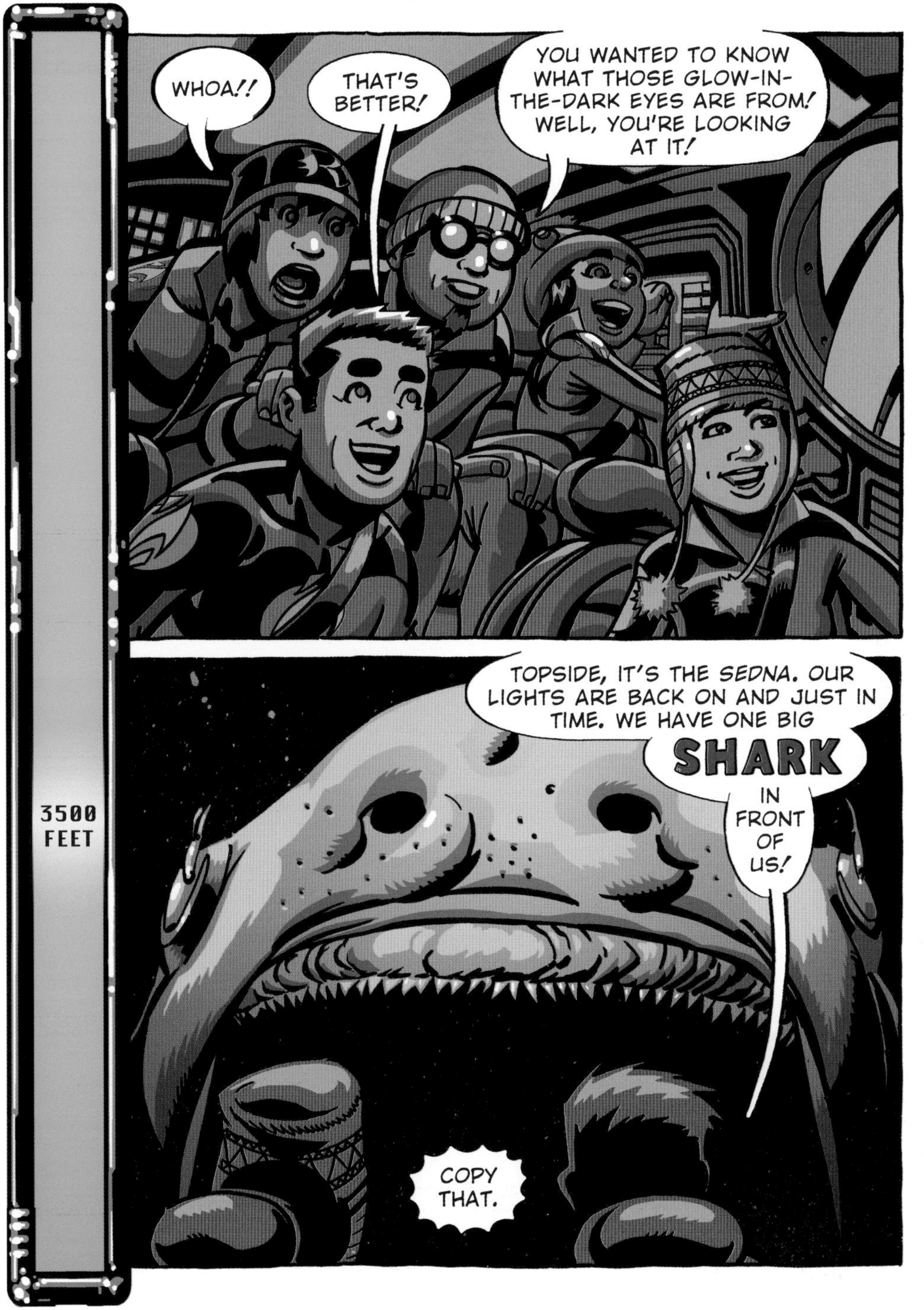

WHOA!!

THAT'S BETTER!

YOU WANTED TO KNOW WHAT THOSE GLOW-IN-THE-DARK EYES ARE FROM! WELL, YOU'RE LOOKING AT IT!

3500 FEET

WHAT KIND OF SHARK IS IT?
IT'S A GREENLAND SHARK.
YOU DON'T NEED TO WORRY ABOUT THIS MONSTER. IT'S RELATIVELY HARMLESS AND SHOULD LEAVE US ALONE.
3500 FEET
THEIR EYES ARE SO COOL-LOOKING.
YES, THEY ARE. HOWEVER, MOST OF THESE SHARKS CAN'T SEE.
WHY NOT?
BECAUSE THEY'VE BEEN BLINDED BY PARASITES, WHICH HANG FROM THEIR EYES. ONE THEORY SUGGESTS THE PARASITES ACT LIKE LURES TO ATTRACT FOOD FOR THE SHARK. WHEN THE PREY GETS CLOSE, THE SHARK SIMPLY INHALES AND IS ABLE TO SUCK FOOD IN FROM 3 FEET AWAY. POOR MANNERS, PERHAPS, BUT EFFECTIVE.

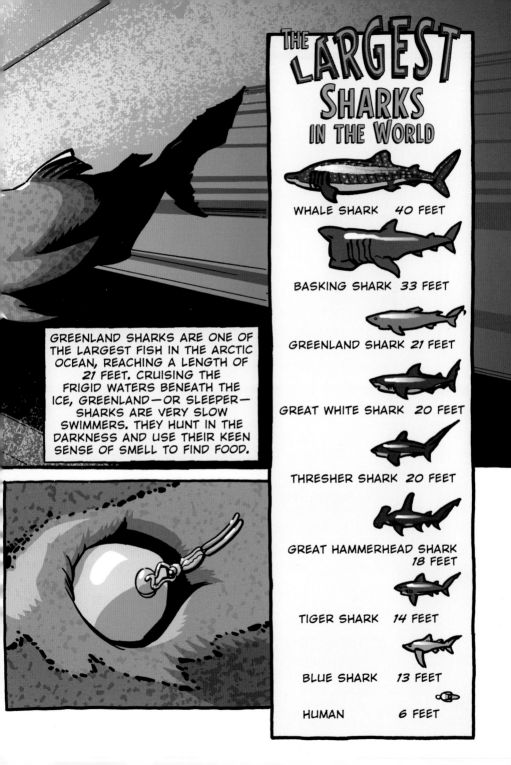

GREENLAND SHARKS ARE ONE OF THE LARGEST FISH IN THE ARCTIC OCEAN, REACHING A LENGTH OF 21 FEET. CRUISING THE FRIGID WATERS BENEATH THE ICE, GREENLAND—OR SLEEPER—SHARKS ARE VERY SLOW SWIMMERS. THEY HUNT IN THE DARKNESS AND USE THEIR KEEN SENSE OF SMELL TO FIND FOOD.

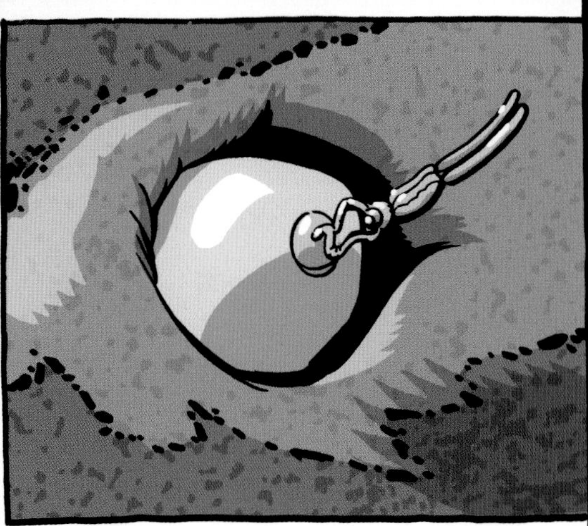

THE LARGEST SHARKS IN THE WORLD

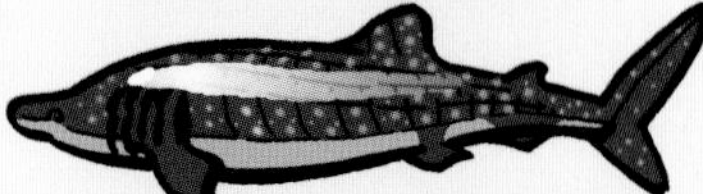

WHALE SHARK 40 FEET

BASKING SHARK 33 FEET

GREENLAND SHARK 21 FEET

GREAT WHITE SHARK 20 FEET

THRESHER SHARK 20 FEET

GREAT HAMMERHEAD SHARK 18 FEET

TIGER SHARK 14 FEET

BLUE SHARK 13 FEET

HUMAN 6 FEET

DAY 4: MARCH 20, 11:26 AM
5000 FEET

WE'RE A LONG WAY DOWN, AT A LEVEL KNOWN AS THE BENTHIC REALM.
WHAT IS THE BENTHIC REALM?
IT'S THE AREA COMPRISED OF ORGANISMS THAT LIVE AT THE BOTTOM OF THE OCEAN.

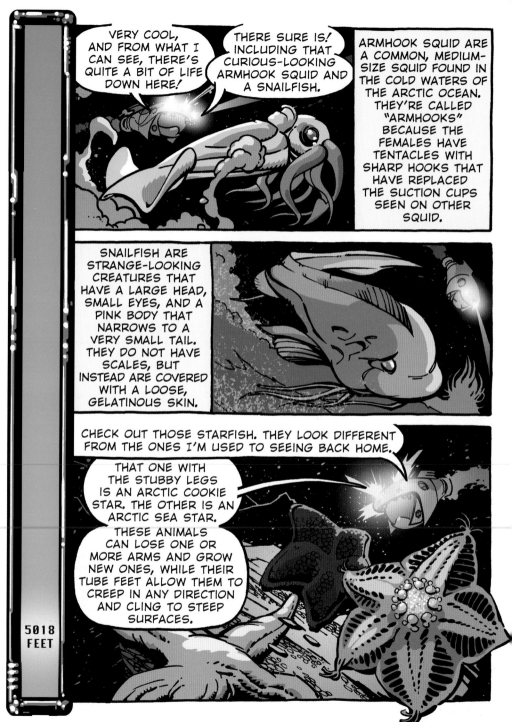

VERY COOL, AND FROM WHAT I CAN SEE, THERE'S QUITE A BIT OF LIFE DOWN HERE!
THERE SURE IS! INCLUDING THAT CURIOUS-LOOKING ARMHOOK SQUID AND A SNAILFISH.
ARMHOOK SQUID ARE A COMMON, MEDIUM-SIZE SQUID FOUND IN THE COLD WATERS OF THE ARCTIC OCEAN. THEY'RE CALLED "ARMHOOKS" BECAUSE THE FEMALES HAVE TENTACLES WITH SHARP HOOKS THAT HAVE REPLACED THE SUCTION CUPS SEEN ON OTHER SQUID.

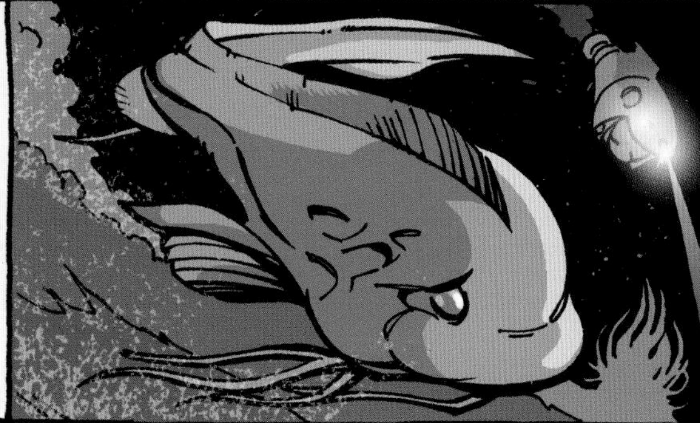
SNAILFISH ARE STRANGE-LOOKING CREATURES THAT HAVE A LARGE HEAD, SMALL EYES, AND A PINK BODY THAT NARROWS TO A VERY SMALL TAIL. THEY DO NOT HAVE SCALES, BUT INSTEAD ARE COVERED WITH A LOOSE, GELATINOUS SKIN.

CHECK OUT THOSE STARFISH. THEY LOOK DIFFERENT FROM THE ONES I'M USED TO SEEING BACK HOME.
THAT ONE WITH THE STUBBY LEGS IS AN ARCTIC COOKIE STAR. THE OTHER IS AN ARCTIC SEA STAR.
THESE ANIMALS CAN LOSE ONE OR MORE ARMS AND GROW NEW ONES, WHILE THEIR TUBE FEET ALLOW THEM TO CREEP IN ANY DIRECTION AND CLING TO STEEP SURFACES.
5018 FEET

TOPSIDE, THIS IS THE *SEDNA*. WE'VE TOUCHED DOWN AT THE BOTTOM. OUR DEPTH IS OVER 5,000 FEET.
THE AVERAGE DEPTH OF THE ARCTIC OCEAN IS 3,406 FEET. THE DEEPEST POINT IS LITKE DEEP AT 17,880 FEET.
COPY, *SEDNA*. WE STILL READ YOU LOUD AND CLEAR. HOW IS IT DOWN THERE?
TRULY AMAZING! ALMOST FEELS LIKE WE'RE ON A SPACE MISSION. WE'LL TURN ON THE VIDEO FEED SO YOU CAN SEE WHAT OUR LIGHTS ARE PICKING UP.
THANK YOU. WE'RE SEEING THE IMAGES NICE AND CLEAR.
HEY, KIDS, DID YOU KNOW EARLY MARINE EXPLORERS BELIEVED LIFE DIDN'T EXIST THIS DEEP? BUT THANKS TO MODERN TECHNOLOGY LIKE OUR SUB AND THE CAMERAS WE JUST TURNED ON, WE KNOW IT DOES.
JUST LOOK AROUND. IT'S REMARKABLE THAT IN A PLACE WHERE SUNLIGHT CANNOT REACH AND PLANTS CANNOT SURVIVE, THE BOTTOM FLOURISHES WITH LIVING CREATURES.
5022 FEET

THIS HAS TO BE THE MOST EXCITING TRIP I'VE EVER TAKEN!
ME TOO! I FEEL LIKE I'M ON ANOTHER PLANET!
FUNNY YOU SAY THAT, OLIVIA. DO YOU KNOW MORE PEOPLE HAVE LANDED ON THE MOON THAN HAVE VISITED THE DEEP ARCTIC OCEAN?
IN FACT, SCIENTISTS KNOW MORE ABOUT MARS THAN WHAT OCCURS AT THESE FRIGID DEPTHS.
AND FEW PEOPLE KNOW THAT THE DEEP-SEA COVERS MORE THAN HALF OUR PLANET.
WE'RE SO LUCKY TO BE SEEING WHAT MOST PEOPLE HAVEN'T.
WE *ARE* LUCKY. THAT'S WHY JOURNEYS LIKE THIS ONE ARE SO IMPORTANT... IT ALLOWS US TO LEARN MORE ABOUT THIS MYSTERIOUS OCEAN AND ALL OF ITS SPECIAL LIFE FORMS...
...AND THEN SHARE OUR DISCOVERIES WITH THE REST OF THE WORLD!
5026 FEET

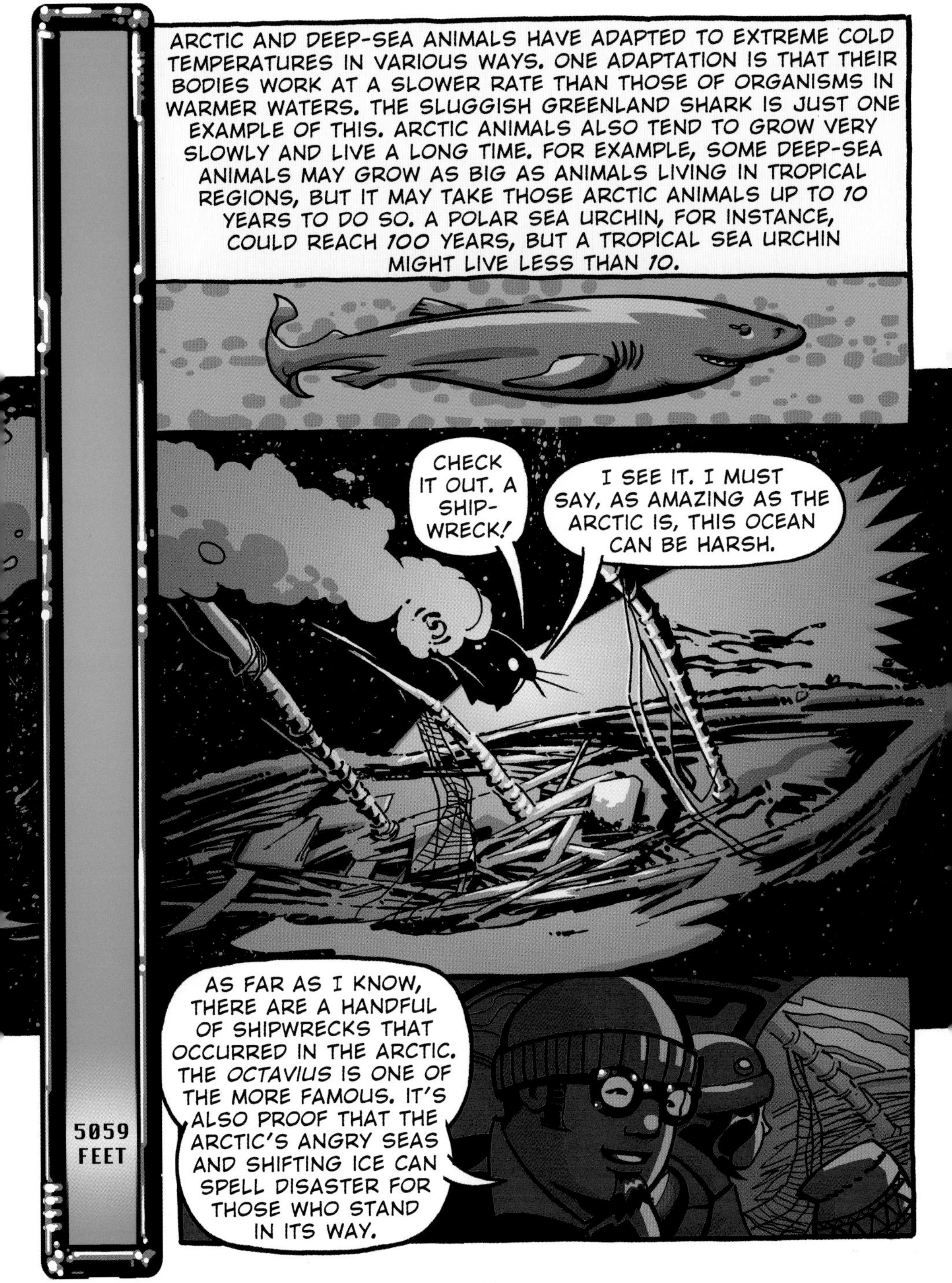

ARCTIC AND DEEP-SEA ANIMALS HAVE ADAPTED TO EXTREME COLD TEMPERATURES IN VARIOUS WAYS. ONE ADAPTATION IS THAT THEIR BODIES WORK AT A SLOWER RATE THAN THOSE OF ORGANISMS IN WARMER WATERS. THE SLUGGISH GREENLAND SHARK IS JUST ONE EXAMPLE OF THIS. ARCTIC ANIMALS ALSO TEND TO GROW VERY SLOWLY AND LIVE A LONG TIME. FOR EXAMPLE, SOME DEEP-SEA ANIMALS MAY GROW AS BIG AS ANIMALS LIVING IN TROPICAL REGIONS, BUT IT MAY TAKE THOSE ARCTIC ANIMALS UP TO 10 YEARS TO DO SO. A POLAR SEA URCHIN, FOR INSTANCE, COULD REACH 100 YEARS, BUT A TROPICAL SEA URCHIN MIGHT LIVE LESS THAN 10.

CHECK IT OUT. A SHIP-WRECK!
I SEE IT. I MUST SAY, AS AMAZING AS THE ARCTIC IS, THIS OCEAN CAN BE HARSH.
AS FAR AS I KNOW, THERE ARE A HANDFUL OF SHIPWRECKS THAT OCCURRED IN THE ARCTIC. THE *OCTAVIUS* IS ONE OF THE MORE FAMOUS. IT'S ALSO PROOF THAT THE ARCTIC'S ANGRY SEAS AND SHIFTING ICE CAN SPELL DISASTER FOR THOSE WHO STAND IN ITS WAY.
5059 FEET

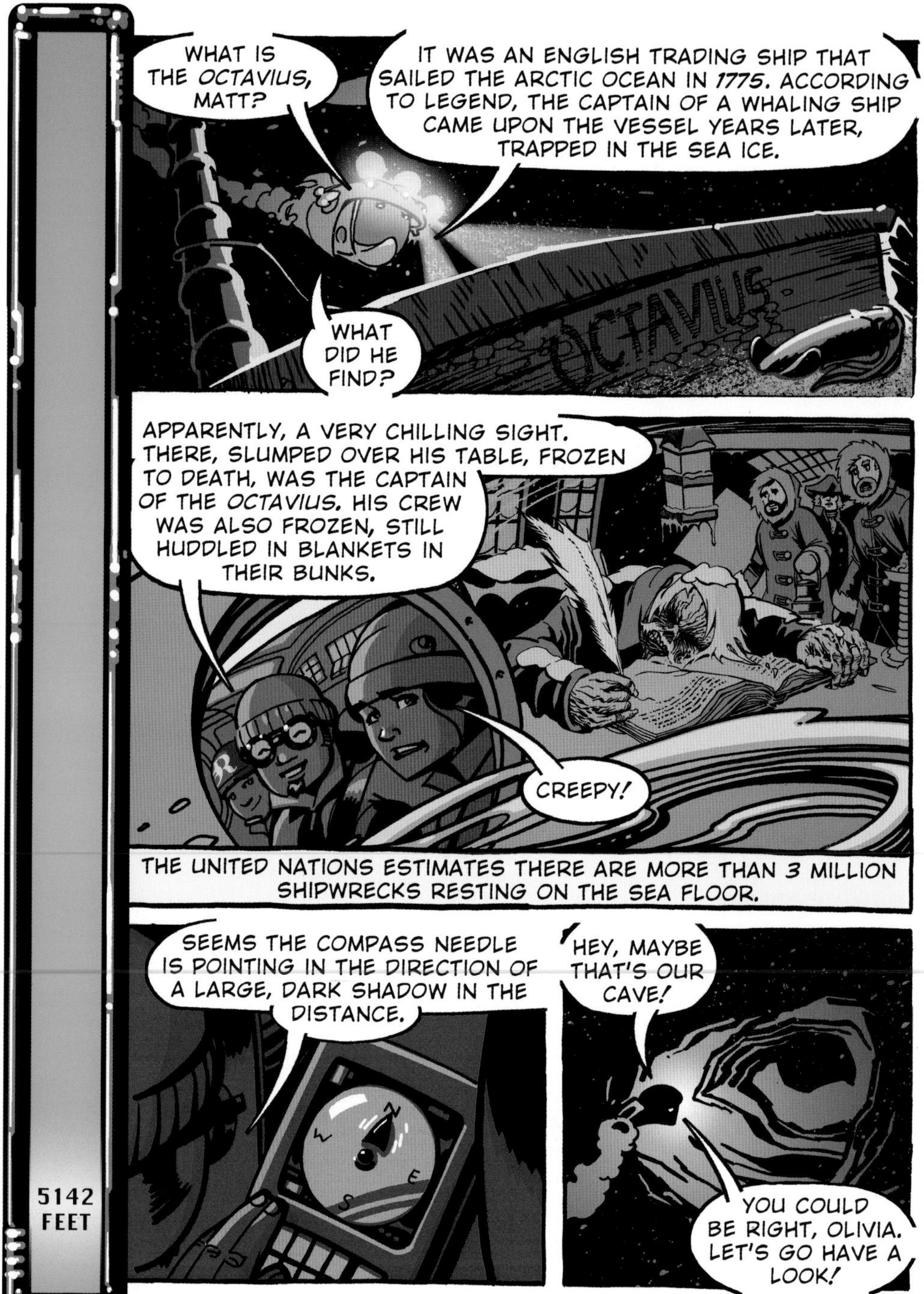

5142 FEET

WHAT IS THE *OCTAVIUS*, MATT?

IT WAS AN ENGLISH TRADING SHIP THAT SAILED THE ARCTIC OCEAN IN *1775*. ACCORDING TO LEGEND, THE CAPTAIN OF A WHALING SHIP CAME UPON THE VESSEL YEARS LATER, TRAPPED IN THE SEA ICE.

OCTAVIUS

WHAT DID HE FIND?

APPARENTLY, A VERY CHILLING SIGHT. THERE, SLUMPED OVER HIS TABLE, FROZEN TO DEATH, WAS THE CAPTAIN OF THE *OCTAVIUS*. HIS CREW WAS ALSO FROZEN, STILL HUDDLED IN BLANKETS IN THEIR BUNKS.

CREEPY!

THE UNITED NATIONS ESTIMATES THERE ARE MORE THAN 3 MILLION SHIPWRECKS RESTING ON THE SEA FLOOR.

SEEMS THE COMPASS NEEDLE IS POINTING IN THE DIRECTION OF A LARGE, DARK SHADOW IN THE DISTANCE.
N
W
E
S

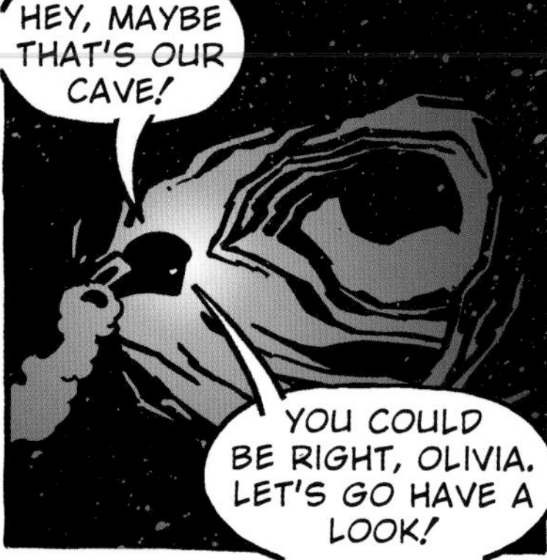

HEY, MAYBE THAT'S OUR CAVE!
YOU COULD BE RIGHT, OLIVIA. LET'S GO HAVE A LOOK!

DAY 4: MARCH 20, 11:40 AM

TOPSIDE, THIS IS THE SEDNA. WE'RE AT 5,307 FEET AND HAVE LOCATED WHAT APPEARS TO BE OUR CAVE.

COPY, SEDNA.

DO YOU HAVE ROOM TO NAVIGATE?

I THINK SO. THE CAVE LOOKS MUCH LARGER THAN IT APPEARS ON THE VIDEO MONITOR.

HOPEFULLY OUR DUMBO OCTOPUS IS SOMEWHERE INSIDE.

5307 FEET

WHAT ARE THOSE CRACKING NOISES I HEAR?
THAT'S THE WATER PRESSURE TIGHTENING AROUND THE SUB.
ARE WE OKAY?
YES, THIS SUB HAS BEEN DESIGNED TO WITHSTAND SUCH EXTREME PRESSURE.
IMAGINE LYING ON THE FLOOR, OLIVIA, AND RESTING A BUCKET OF WATER ON YOUR STOMACH.
THAT'S HEAVY!
YES, IT IS, BUT NOW IMAGINE MORE THAN 3,000 BUCKETS OF WATER ALL PRESSING ON YOU AT THE SAME TIME. THAT'S WHAT IT'S LIKE THIS DEEP. FORTUNATELY, WE'RE INSIDE A PRESSURIZED SUB, SO WE DON'T FEEL A THING.
THAT'S GOOD TO KNOW.
THE DARK, COLD WATER DOWN HERE IS ALSO VERY LOW IN OXYGEN, WHICH MEANS LIFE THIS DEEP REQUIRES VERY LITTLE TO SURVIVE.
LIKE OUR DUMBO OCTOPUS?
YES. THE DUMBO OCTOPUS, LIKE MANY OTHER DEEP-SEA CREATURES, CONSERVES ITS ENERGY BY OFTEN REMAINING IN ONE PLACE AND AMBUSHING ITS PREY, SUCH AS SNAILS AND WORMS, AS THEY SWIM BY.
5311 FEET

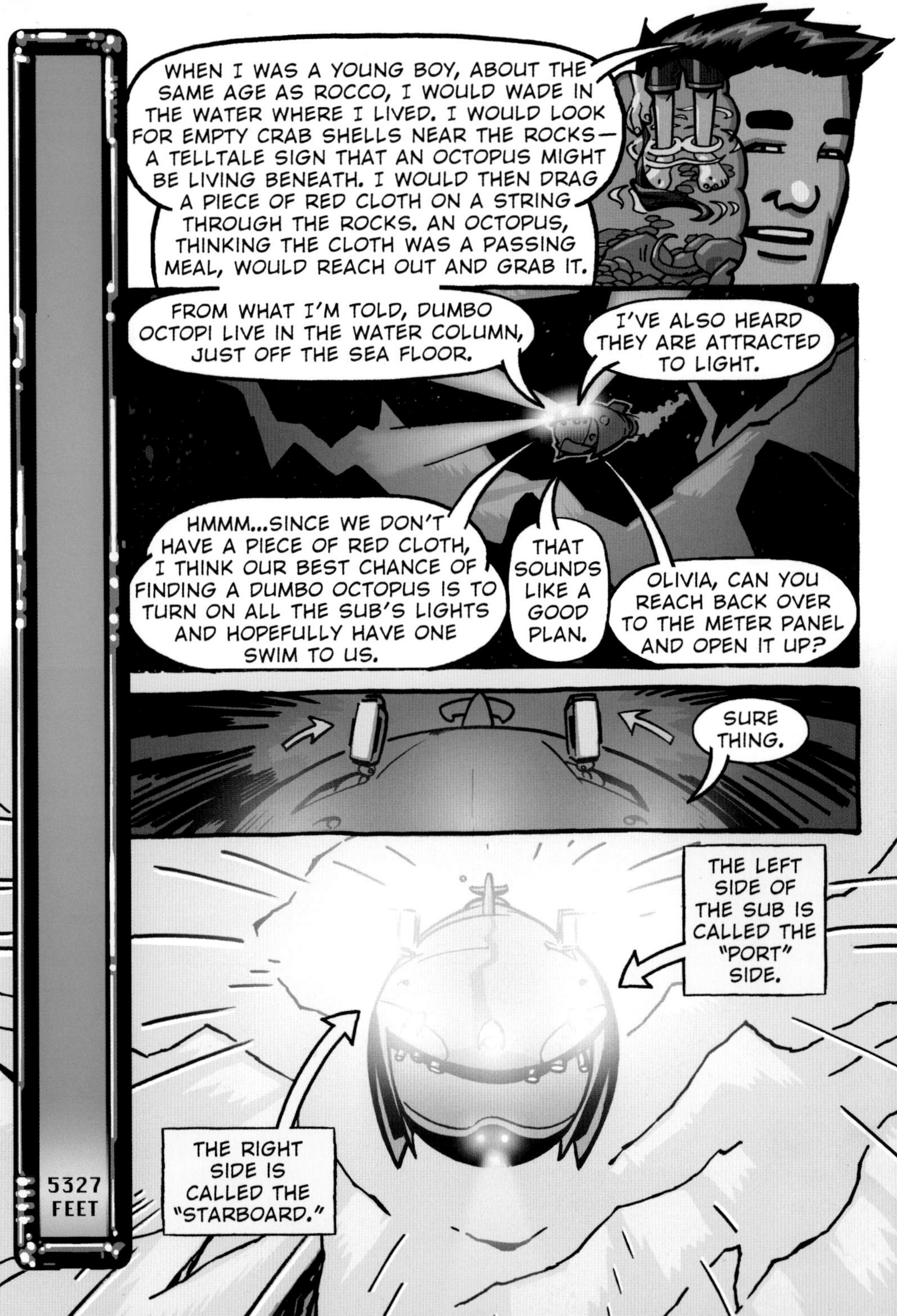

WHEN I WAS A YOUNG BOY, ABOUT THE SAME AGE AS ROCCO, I WOULD WADE IN THE WATER WHERE I LIVED. I WOULD LOOK FOR EMPTY CRAB SHELLS NEAR THE ROCKS— A TELLTALE SIGN THAT AN OCTOPUS MIGHT BE LIVING BENEATH. I WOULD THEN DRAG A PIECE OF RED CLOTH ON A STRING THROUGH THE ROCKS. AN OCTOPUS, THINKING THE CLOTH WAS A PASSING MEAL, WOULD REACH OUT AND GRAB IT.
FROM WHAT I'M TOLD, DUMBO OCTOPI LIVE IN THE WATER COLUMN, JUST OFF THE SEA FLOOR.
I'VE ALSO HEARD THEY ARE ATTRACTED TO LIGHT.
HMMM...SINCE WE DON'T HAVE A PIECE OF RED CLOTH, I THINK OUR BEST CHANCE OF FINDING A DUMBO OCTOPUS IS TO TURN ON ALL THE SUB'S LIGHTS AND HOPEFULLY HAVE ONE SWIM TO US.
THAT SOUNDS LIKE A GOOD PLAN.
OLIVIA, CAN YOU REACH BACK OVER TO THE METER PANEL AND OPEN IT UP?
SURE THING.
THE LEFT SIDE OF THE SUB IS CALLED THE "PORT" SIDE.
THE RIGHT SIDE IS CALLED THE "STARBOARD."
5327 FEET

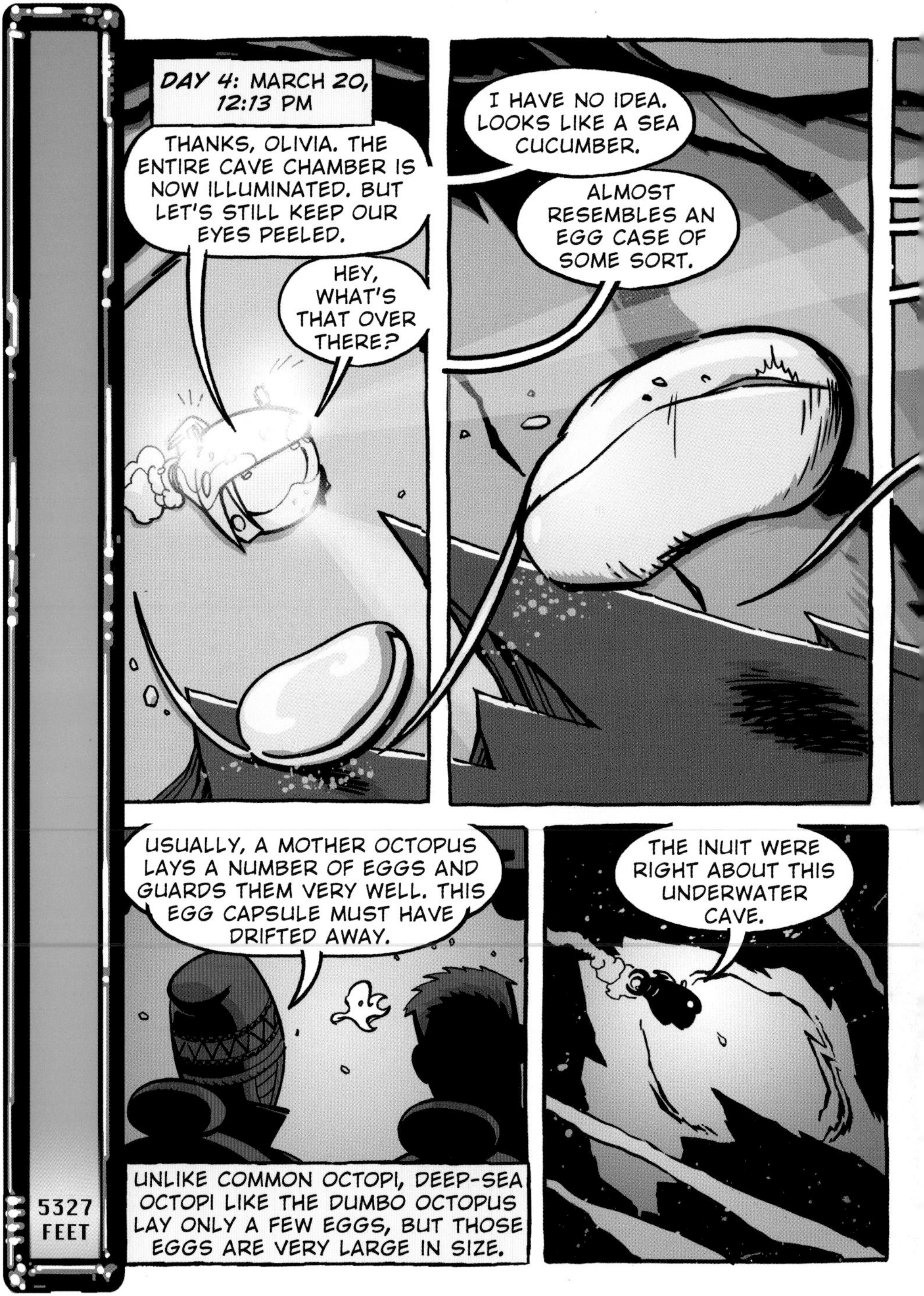

DAY 4: MARCH 20, 12:13 PM

THANKS, OLIVIA. THE ENTIRE CAVE CHAMBER IS NOW ILLUMINATED. BUT LET'S STILL KEEP OUR EYES PEELED.

HEY, WHAT'S THAT OVER THERE?

USUALLY, A MOTHER OCTOPUS LAYS A NUMBER OF EGGS AND GUARDS THEM VERY WELL. THIS EGG CAPSULE MUST HAVE DRIFTED AWAY.

UNLIKE COMMON OCTOPI, DEEP-SEA OCTOPI LIKE THE DUMBO OCTOPUS LAY ONLY A FEW EGGS, BUT THOSE EGGS ARE VERY LARGE IN SIZE.

5327 FEET

I THINK IT'S AN EGG CAPSULE.
I JUST SAW SOMETHING MOVE INSIDE!
ME TOO.
OH MY GOSH! IT'S A BABY DUMBO OCTOPUS!
AND THEY WERE RIGHT ABOUT THE DUMBO OCTOPUS!
THEY SURE WERE.
NOW, ALL WE HAVE TO DO IS CATCH OUR LITTLE FRIEND.
THIS DUMBO OCTOPUS, AN OCTOPOD WITH THE SCIENTIFIC NAME *CIRROTEUTHIS MUELLERI*, IS COMMON IN THE ARCTIC, AROUND GREENLAND, AND FOUND IN BOTH THE NORTH ATLANTIC AND NORTH PACIFIC OCEANS. IT FALLS INTO THE CATEGORY OF UMBRELLA OCTOPUS BECAUSE OF THE WEBBING BETWEEN ITS ARMS. WHEN IT IS STRETCHED OUT, IT RESEMBLES AN OPEN UMBRELLA.

DUMBO OCTOPI ARE THE DEEPEST-DWELLING AMONG ALL OCTOPI. THEIR LIFESPAN IS TYPICALLY BETWEEN 3 TO 5 YEARS.
SEDNA, THIS IS TOPSIDE. BE CAREFUL. WE DON'T LIKE WHAT WE ARE SEEING.
COPY, TOPSIDE.
WHAT DO YOU WANT TO DO, FABIEN?
I WOULD LIKE TO CATCH OUR LITTLE FRIEND...
LET'S TRY TO DO THIS QUICK.
I AGREE WITH MATT.
ROCCO, CAN YOU REACH THE SCIENCE PANEL JUST OVER MATT'S RIGHT SHOULDER?
YES, I CAN.
GREAT! OPEN THE PANEL AND YOU'LL SEE A SWITCH MARKED "SUCTION SAMPLER." PLEASE FLIP IT TO THE ON POSITION.
WILL DO!
5349 FEET

WHAT'S A SUCTION SAMPLER?
IT'S BASICALLY AN UNDERWATER VACUUM THAT COLLECTS CREATURES BY GENTLY SUCKING THEM INTO A TUBE AND DEPOSITING THEM INTO A COLLECTION BUCKET.
IT'S ONE OF THE TOOLS WE HAVE ONBOARD TO COLLECT SEMIFRAGILE ANIMALS FROM THE DEEP, LIKE THE DUMBO OCTOPUS.
WE CALL IT THE "CRITTER GETTER."
VERY COOL!
OKAY, IT'S ON!
THANKS, ROCCO!
5358 FEET

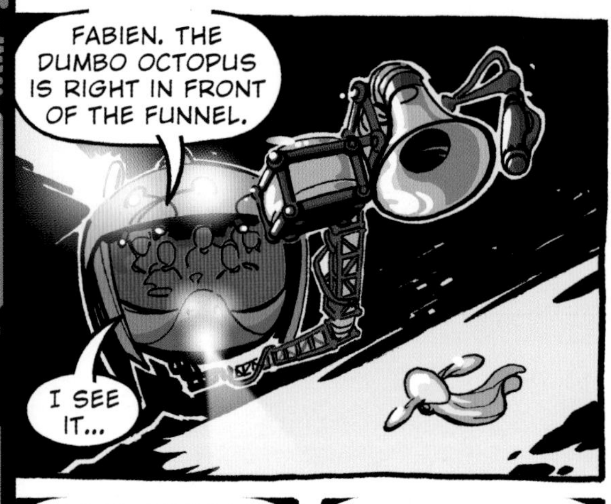

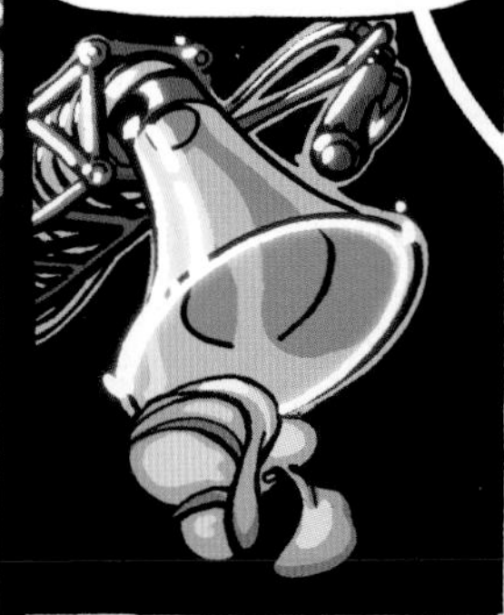

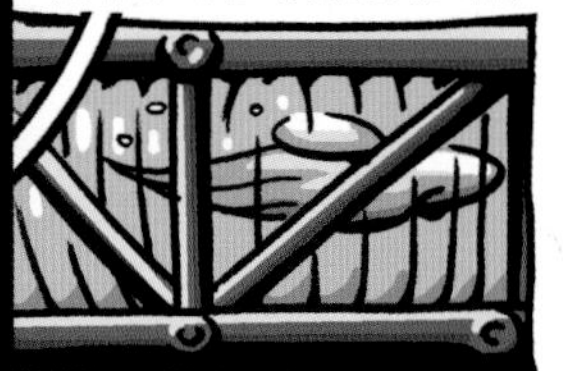

THANKS, MATT.

5372 FEET

COPY, SEDNA. WE ADVISE THAT YOU EXIT THE CAVE IMMEDIATELY AND RETURN TO THE SURFACE.
5095 FEET
WILL DO, TOPSIDE. HOPEFULLY THE ICE HASN'T SHIFTED AND COVERED OUR EXIT HOLE.
1067 FEET
85 FEET
COPY...THE ICE IS MOVING, BUT THE HOLE IS STILL LARGE ENOUGH FOR YOU TO SURFACE.
OKAY, TOPSIDE. WE'RE HEADING UP...

DAY 4: MARCH 20, 1:09 PM
DURING THE SEDNA'S DESCENT, THE ICE HAD SHIFTED AGAIN, FREEING THE TRAPPED BOWHEAD WHALE WHILE FORMING A LARGER HOLE IN THE ICE.
SNOW SERPENT

SNOW SERPENT'S COLD ROOM

WHY IS IT SO COLD IN HERE?

IT'S SO WE CAN KEEP DEEP-SEA ANIMALS LIKE OUR DUMBO OCTOPUS NEAR THE SAME TEMPERATURE THAT THEY EXPERIENCE IN THE WILD.

THINK OF THIS ROOM AS A WALK-IN REFRIGERATOR, WHICH IS NOT EASY TO WORK IN. THESE NEAR FREEZING TEMPERATURES MAKE IT HARD TO STAY ALERT, BUT IT'S ALL IN THE NAME OF SCIENCE.

FABIEN, IF YOU DON'T MIND, I WOULD LIKE TO STAY BEHIND AND BEGIN MY OBSERVATIONS BEFORE WE LET OUR LITTLE FRIEND GO FREE.
ABSOLUTELY.
WHAT OBSERVATIONS ARE YOU GOING TO MAKE, GLORIA?
WELL, FIRST I WILL EXPLORE THE DIFFERENT WAYS THE DUMBO OCTOPUS FINDS ITS FOOD.

THEN I'LL TEST THE ANIMAL'S INTELLIGENCE COMPARED TO SHALLOW-WATER OCTOPI TO SEE IF THE DUMBO CHANGES COLOR, SKIN, TEXTURE, AND POSTURE WHEN IT'S ANGRY, CONFUSED, OR SCARED.
IN LABORATORY EXPERIMENTS, OCTOPI CAN BE TRAINED TO DISTINGUISH BETWEEN DIFFERENT SHAPES AND PATTERNS.

WHY IS IT IMPORTANT TO CONDUCT DIFFERENT EXPERIMENTS?
REMEMBER WHAT WE SHARED WITH YOU AT THE BEGINNING OF THIS EXPEDITION, ROCCO.

BECAUSE THESE AMAZING CREATURES HAVE LEARNED TO SURVIVE IN SUCH A COLD, DARK, AND HOSTILE PLACE AS THE ARCTIC, WE'RE HOPING THEY MAY HELP US ONE DAY TO ADAPT AND SURVIVE IN SIMILAR ENVIRONMENTS.
OH, THAT'S RIGHT!

I WOULD LIKE TO KNOW IF WE CAN SURVIVE IN ENVIRONMENTS LIKE THE ARCTIC.
ME TOO!

DAY 5: MARCH 21, 4:47 PM

THIS HAS BEEN SO EXCITING, THANK YOU, FABIEN!

YES, THANK YOU FOR INVITING US TO JOIN YOU!

OF COURSE, AND THANK YOU BOTH FOR YOUR HELP, ESPECIALLY INSIDE THE SUB. I HOPE THIS EXPEDITION WAS AS EXCITING AND EDUCATIONAL FOR YOU AS IT HAS BEEN FOR US.

IT WAS, FOR SURE!

ARCTIC COD

EDIBLE SEAWEED

BANNOCK (INUIT BREAD)

DUCK SOUP

THE INUIT DRUM IS CALLED A *QILAUT* AND IS TRADITIONALLY MADE FROM CARIBOU SKIN WITH SEAL OR WALRUS SKIN AROUND THE HANDLE.

WELL, LIVING IN THE EXTREME COLD ALLOWS THEM TO KEEP THEIR FOOD FROZEN ALL YEAR ROUND, UNTIL IT'S READY TO EAT, WHICH MEANS A LOT LESS SPOILAGE. FOR US, WE HAVE TO FREEZE OUR FOOD IN FREEZERS, WHICH CONSUME *10* TIMES MORE ENERGY THAN NOT USING A FREEZER. THE INUIT ALSO FISH, HUNT, OR COLLECT MUCH OF THEIR FOOD CLOSE BY. FOR US, THE AVERAGE MEAL TRAVELS MORE THAN *1,000* MILES TO REACH OUR DINNER TABLE.

FABIEN, AS YOU KNOW, THE ICE IN THE ARCTIC IS MELTING VERY FAST, AND SOON TRADITIONAL SKILLS LIKE THE BUILDING OF A SNOW HOUSE WILL BE LOST FOREVER.

THE MELTING ICE IS ALSO DESTROYING OUR ABILITY TO HUNT, BECAUSE OUR ANIMALS ARE VANISHING QUICKER THAN EVER.

WE FEAR OUR CHILDREN WILL NOT ONLY LOSE THEIR TRADITIONAL SKILLS, BUT THEY WILL BE UNABLE TO FEED THEIR CHILDREN.

I SYMPATHIZE WITH YOUR CONCERNS. AS YOU'VE SEEN IN THE LAST 35 YEARS, THE ARCTIC SEA ICE HAS DECLINED BY ALMOST HALF BECAUSE OF THE LARGE AMOUNT OF CARBON DIOXIDE THAT'S BEEN EMITTED INTO THE AIR. AND WITH THE LOSS OF ICE, THE ANIMALS YOU RELY ON FOR FOOD AND CLOTHING ARE SPENDING MORE ENERGY LOCATING PREY. THIS LEADS TO FEWER ANIMALS BEING BORN EACH YEAR.
WHICH IS WHY HUNTING HAS BEEN SO DIFFICULT.
I'M SURE YOU REMEMBER SEEING MANY WALRUS AND POLAR BEARS USING THE SEA ICE TO REST AND WARM THEMSELVES. BUT LESS ICE NOW MEANS FEWER RESTING PLACES AND FEWER OPPORTUNITIES FOR THESE ANIMALS TO CAPTURE THEIR FOOD.
THAT IS TRUE. THE POLAR BEARS NOW RUN TO ANYTHING THEY SEE MOVING ON THE ICE, HOPING IT WILL LEAD TO A MEAL.
SOME SCIENTISTS BELIEVE THE ARCTIC MAY BECOME ICE FREE FOR THE FIRST TIME IN HUMAN HISTORY BY 2040.

WE SAW THAT FIRST-HAND WHEN WE WERE IN OUR SUBMARINE. THEY CAME RUNNING EVERY TIME.
THE BEARS LOOKED VERY THIN. I'VE NEVER SEEN SUCH SKINNY POLAR BEARS.
THEY ARE SLOWLY STARVING... AND SOON, WE WILL BE TOO.
I'M SURE ALL OF YOU ARE FEELING THE EFFECTS TOO, WHERE YOU LIVE.
WE ARE. AS MORE ICE MELTS, LESS ENERGY IS REFLECTED INTO SPACE, AND MORE IS ABSORBED BY THE OCEAN. THIS, IN TURN, MAKES THE SEAS WARMER, WHICH MELTS THE ICE EVEN MORE. IT IS A VICIOUS CIRCLE. THE ONLY WAY TO STOP THE ICE FROM MELTING IS TO PROTECT AND HELP THE ENVIRONMENT.
DURING OUR VOYAGE, WE LISTED A NUMBER OF WAYS WE CAN DO OUR PART BACK HOME TO FIGHT AGAINST CLIMATE CHANGE.
SOME ACTIVITIES SEEM VERY EASY TO DO, LIKE WASH OUR CLOTHES IN COLD WATER OR WALK MORE AND DRIVE LESS.
THAT'S RIGHT. AND IF WE ALL HELP, THIS GREAT PLANET AND ALL OF ITS MAGICAL TREASURES, LIKE THE DUMBO OCTOPUS, WILL CONTINUE TO FLOURISH FOR GENERATIONS TO COME.
AS ONE OF OUR INUIT CHIEFS ONCE SAID TO US: "LAND IS NOT SOMETHING YOU OWN. LAND IS A GIFT THAT YOU USE TO LIVE... PROTECT IT AND LOOK AFTER IT. FOREVER."

DAY 5: MARCH 21, 7:07 PM
BEFORE WE DEPART IN THE MORNING, A TRUE MUST ON ANY POLAR EXPEDITION IS THE POLAR PLUNGE.
WHAT IS THE POLAR PLUNGE?
IT'S WHERE WE JUMP INTO THE ARCTIC OCEAN!

ARE YOU CRAZY?! NO WAY!!
THINK OF IT AS AN INVIGORATING SWIM THAT LASTS ONLY SECONDS.
I'M SORRY, BUT THAT WATER IS FREEZING!
NOT QUITE. IT'S ACTUALLY A TOASTY 34 DEGREES RIGHT NOW.

THAT'S COMFORTING, FABIEN.
ON SECOND THOUGHT, WE SHOULD DO IT, ROCCO. WE MAY REGRET THIS FOR THE REST OF OUR LIVES IF WE DON'T.

OKAY, ON THE COUNT OF THREE, WE'LL DISROBE, JUMP IN THE WATER, THEN LET THE CURRENT CARRY US OVER TO THE NEXT GANGWAY TO CLIMB OUT!

MY NERVES ARE FREAKING OUT RIGHT NOW!

I CAN FEEL MY HEART RACING! THIS IS FOR THE TRULY INSANE!

OKAY...THREE, TWO, ONE...

LET'S GO!!

HERE'S TO OUR SUCCESSFUL MISSION!

AND TO A SAFE AND JOYOUS POLAR PLUNGE!

CHEERS!!

THE END

The author and artist would like to thank the wonderfully talented editorial-publishing team at Margaret K. McElderry Books and Simon & Schuster Children's Publishing, including Karen Wojtyla, Sonia Chaghatzbanian, Tom Daly, and Nicole Fiorica; Paul Zemitzsch and Explore Green; David Tanguay and Sonya Pelletier for their coloring assistance; and Professor Jean-Michel Huctin and the Research Centre CEARC from the University of Versailles Saint-Quentin-en-Yvelines, France, for his review of Inuit traditions and culture.

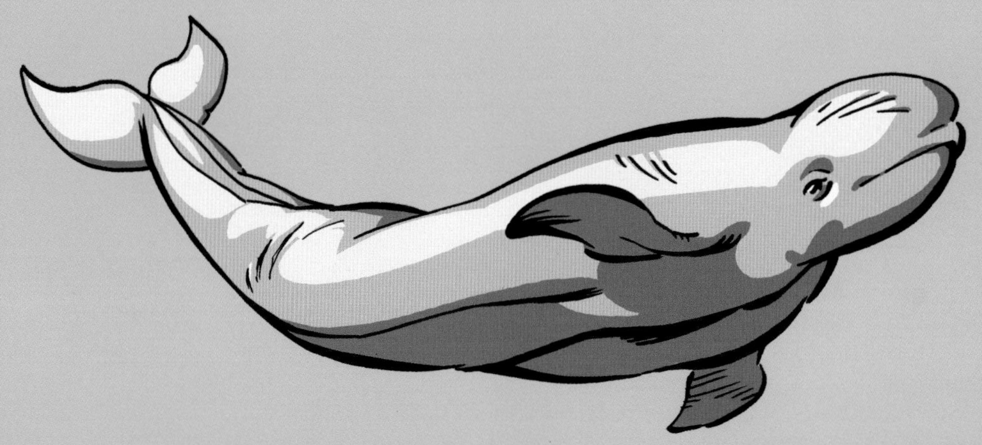

FABIEN COUSTEAU is the grandson of famed sea explorer Jacques Cousteau and a third generation ocean explorer and filmmaker. He has worked with National Geographic, Discovery, PBS, and CBS to produce ocean exploration documentaries, and continues to produce environmentally oriented content for schools, books, magazines, and newspapers. Learn more about his work at fabiencousteauolc.org.

JAMES O. FRAIOLI is a published author of twenty-five books and an award-winning filmmaker. He has traveled the globe alongside experienced guides, naturalists, and scientists, and has spent considerable time exploring and writing about the outdoors. He has served on the board of directors for the Seattle Aquarium and works with many environmental organizations. Learn more about his work at vesperentertainment.com.

JOE ST.PIERRE has sold over two million comic books illustrating and writing for Marvel, DC, and Valiant Comics, among others. Joe also works in the fields of intellectual property design, commercial illustration, and storyboards for animation and video games. Joe's publishing company, Astronaut Ink, highlights his creator-owned properties Bold Blood, Megahurtz®, and the sold out New Zodiax. See his work at astronautink.com and popartproperties.com.